tiger's-eye

tiger's-eye

Belinda Ray

SCHOLASTIC INC.
New York Toronto London Auckland Sydney
Mexico City New Delhi Hong Kong Buenos Aires

For my mother, an avid reader and solver of crossword puzzles who gave me the gift of words.—B.R.

ISBN 0-439-77514-0

ALLOYENTERTAINMENT Produced by Alloy Entertainment
151 West 26th Street, New York, NY 10001

12 11 10 9 8 7 6 5 4 3 2   5 6 7 8 9 10/0

Printed in the U.S.A.   40
First printing, October 2005

CHAPTER
One

Dear Jasmine,

I was thinking . . . you may be in NH, but you're still only two and half hours away from Boston. Maybe I could come up and visit you sometime. Like right now. *Homeroom is soooo boring. Remember that e-mail I sent you about my teacher, Mrs. MacKnight? The strictest teacher in the whole school? Turns out she's the boring-est, too. Emily and Sarah are so lucky. They're probably playing games in Ms. Garcia's room right now while I'm stuck here—*

"Miss Johnson?"

Keisha jumped at the sound of her name. "Y-yes?"

"Are you *taking* notes or *writing* them?" Mrs.

MacKnight asked, peering over the top of her horn-rimmed glasses.

"Um, taking notes?" Keisha replied. It came out more like a question than an answer.

Mrs. MacKnight squinted skeptically. "I'll take your word for it," she said, "this time. But do sit up straight. Poor posture is a sign of laziness."

Keisha stretched upward, making her spine as straight as possible.

"And, Mr. Hunter," Mrs. MacKnight barked. "I expect you to stay in your seat until the bell rings."

Jesse Hunter, who sat in front of Keisha, had started to rise, but he immediately lowered himself back into his chair. At the same time, Keisha took the note she'd been writing to her friend Jasmine, who'd moved away five months ago, and stuffed it into her backpack. The last thing she wanted was for Mrs. MacKnight to take it from her and read it to the entire class.

"Thank you," Mrs. MacKnight said when Jesse was settled. She pushed her glasses farther up on her angular nose and surveyed the classroom. Apparently, no one was looking too lazy because she gave a slight, tight-lipped smile and continued with the afternoon announcements.

"Soccer tryouts will be held at two-thirty on the . . . oh, pardon me. That's only for seventh and eighth graders." She scanned the paper she was holding in her slim hands, then set it carefully down on her desk blotter. "It appears that we've reached the end of the announcements for today. I, however, have one more of my own."

She stood away from her desk, smoothed the pleats on the front of her long black skirt, and picked up a stack of 4" x 6" index cards. She passed them out as she spoke, and then she returned to the front of the room. "For homework, I would like you all to fill out these cards by completing the following sentences. Number one: My personal goals for this school year are—. Number two: My academic goals for this school year are—. And number three: One skill at which I would like to improve this year is—."

This has to be a joke, Keisha thought as she scrambled to write all of the sentences on her card. Homework for *homeroom?* Who ever heard of such a thing?

"Please include your full name, last name first, at the top of your card," Mrs. MacKnight continued, "and be ready to hand them in first thing tomorrow morning. Students who neglect to bring in their cards will report to my room during lunch to complete them."

Unbelievable, Keisha thought, still scribbling. She paused to tuck a stray strand of dark, curly hair back behind her ear. In another month it would be long enough to stay in a low ponytail all day—if she could last that long without cutting it all off. Her friends were always telling her how much they envied her voluminous hair, but Keisha seemed to spend half her time trying to smooth it out and the other half wishing she had long, straight hair like theirs.

Both Sarah and Emily had brown hair that fell a few inches below their shoulders. From behind, it would be hard to tell them apart, except that Sarah often wore her hair either half up or in a ponytail while Emily, whose hair was a shade darker, mostly wore hers down.

Keisha ran a hand across the top of her head, making sure she didn't have any renegade hairs going crazy up there, and wondered what Sarah and Emily were doing in their homeroom. So far this week they'd used the ten-minute block at the end of the day to play a game of charades, sample Ms. Garcia's homemade cinnamon-and-sugar cookies, and listen to their favorite songs on Ms. Garcia's iPod. Mrs. MacKnight, on the other hand, had used the time to go over the student handbook and each and every one of the school rules—as well as her personal homeroom rules—in detail. It hardly seemed fair.

"Please use your best cursive handwriting," Mrs. MacKnight instructed. "Mastering a clear, fluid cursive hand is more than a manner in which to develop your fine motor skills. It is an exercise in patience and discipline for your mind as well."

Groans echoed through the classroom, and numerous students—including Keisha—requested new index cards so they could start over. During the remaining three minutes of school, Mrs. MacKnight walked through the rows of desks, fielding questions such as "How do you spell *council*, like *student* council?" and "What's an academic goal?" Meanwhile, Keisha sat hunched over her index card with her tongue sticking out the right side of her mouth, trying desperately to get everything down while keeping her a's from looking like o's and her o's from looking like v's. By the time the bell rang, she had a first-rate hand cramp, a renewed hatred of cursive writing, and another Mrs. MacKnight story to share with her friends.

"You'll never believe what Mrs. MacKnight is making us do," she said to Emily and Sarah when she finally tracked them down at their lockers. That was another stroke of bad luck this year. Not only had Keisha wound up in a different homeroom from her two best friends, but locker assignments were alphabetical, which meant that Sarah Robbins and Emily Reisman were practically side by side while Keisha Johnson was stuck down at the other end of the hall.

"What?" Emily asked, without looking up. She was busy stuffing books into her backpack and she seemed to be in a hurry.

"We have homeroom homework," Keisha said. "Can you believe that?"

"*Homeroom* homework?" Sarah echoed. "That's nasty."

"That's Mrs. MacKnight," Keisha replied. "She's so strict, it's insane. When Jesse Hunter—"

"Did you hear what Jenna called her today?" Emily interrupted as she closed her locker door.

Keisha stared blankly. What did Jenna have to do with anything? Then she glanced at Sarah, who had started to giggle, and realized that Emily wasn't even talking to her. Apparently, she was making a reference that only Sarah understood.

"Didn't she call her Mrs. Mac*Fright*?" Sarah asked.

"Mm-hm," Emily nodded, laughing.

Keisha rolled her eyes. "That's what the sixth graders called Mrs. MacKnight last year," she said, but neither Emily nor Sarah seemed to hear her. They were too busy gushing about how cool and funny Jenna was. Keisha just crossed her arms and waited. It was the only thing she could do.

Jenna Scott was the most popular girl at Adams Middle School. Even though she was only in sixth grade, seventh- and eighth-grade girls invited her to their slumber parties, and seventh- and eighth-grade boys flirted with her like crazy. Sixth graders mostly looked up to her, wanting to be her friend, wanting to be her boyfriend, or just plain wanting to be her. And ever since the beginning of school, Jenna had been Emily and Sarah's favorite topic of conversation.

Not only had they wound up sitting next to her in homeroom, they had also been put into groups with her in math and science, and apparently they were all becoming pretty good friends. *During* classes, anyway. At lunch and after school, Sarah and Emily still hung with Keisha and acted like normal human beings instead of the co-presidents of the Jenna Scott fan club.

"Isn't that awesome?" Emily said, after explaining how Jenna had shot down Derek Pierce when he'd asked her out.

"Yeah, that's great," Keisha said, trying to sound interested, but secretly hoping they were just about done giving her the Jenna play-by-play. Keisha watched as Emily and Sarah finished loading up their backpacks, and decided that it was safe to move on to other topics. Finally. "Are you guys just about ready to go?" she asked. "The movie starts at two-fifty, so if we catch the number nine bus, we should be able to. . ." Keisha let her voice trail off when she noticed that both of her friends were shifting their weight uncomfortably and avoiding making eye contact with her. "What's wrong?"

"Um, well," Sarah started. She glanced nervously at Emily, and the two of them exchanged a look that made Keisha uncomfortable. It was as though they were whispering about her without actually whispering.

"We can't go," Emily said after a moment. She hefted her backpack onto her right shoulder and faced Keisha directly. "We're going over to Jenna's house. She invited us to go swimming in her pool."

"What? When?"

"Yesterday," Sarah said sheepishly. "We were going to tell you, but we didn't know how."

"We didn't want you to think we were ditching you or anything," Emily said. "I mean, we can still go to the movie, just . . . another time, you know?"

"Yeah, sure," Keisha said, although she wasn't sure at all. They may not have wanted to ditch her, but it sure felt like she was being ditched.

"Keisha? Are you mad?" Sarah asked.

"No," Keisha lied. "I just . . . I didn't even know Jenna had a pool."

"Yeah," Sarah nodded, "and it's heated, too, so it's still really warm and everything."

"Plus, it's Olympic size," Emily added. "With two diving boards and two slides."

"Wow," Keisha said. "That sounds . . . great." She tried to smile, but at the same time her shoulders slumped forward a bit. She wasn't trying to look pathetic, but she knew she must from the way her friends were watching her—like she was a stray puppy that they couldn't bring home.

"We're really sorry, Keisha," Sarah said. "I know we said we'd come by your mom's shop and hang out this afternoon, but when Jenna asked us over . . . I mean—how could we turn her down?"

You could have said no, Keisha thought, but at the same time she knew what Sarah meant. People didn't say no to Jenna Scott—at least, not people who wanted to have a shot at being popular at Adams Middle School.

"We'd ask you to come, Keish," Sarah said, "but . . ."

"It's Jenna's house, you know?" Emily put in. "It's not like we can just . . ."

" . . . invite someone else along," Sarah finished.

"Oh, yeah, totally," Keisha said, doing her best to sound upbeat. "I understand. It's no big deal."

"Really?" Emily asked.

"Sure," Keisha lied. "Have a good time."

"Thanks."

Keisha watched her friends as they glanced at their feet, their lockers, the walls—everything around them except Keisha. "Maybe you guys can hang out at the shop tomorrow," Keisha suggested. "I'm helping out all afternoon, but I'm sure my mom would let me take an ice-cream break."

"Yeah, maybe," Sarah said.

"I'll call you when I get home," Emily added.

The three friends stood together for a moment in awkward silence, surrounded by the noise of lockers slamming and voices chattering.

"Well . . . we've gotta go," Emily said finally. "Jenna's waiting for us out front. Her mom's picking us up."

"Oh. Okay. I'll talk to you later," Keisha said.

"Yeah, later," Emily and Sarah replied as they headed down the hall. Keisha watched them go, realizing as they turned the corner that she had been holding her breath. When she let it go, she became aware of burning sensation in her eyes—tears were beginning to form.

Get a grip, Keisha, she told herself. *It's just one afternoon.* It wasn't like Sarah and Emily would be going swimming at Jenna's every day or anything. It was the end of September. Heated or not, all of the outdoor pools in Brookline, Massachusetts, would be shutting down for the winter soon enough. It was probably just a one-time thing.

After all, Jenna Scott had plenty of other friends to hang out with—older friends, more popular friends . . . *cooler* friends. Keisha chastised herself for thinking of it that way. Emily and Sarah were definitely cool enough to hang out with Jenna Scott, or anyone else for that matter. But she couldn't help it. Part of her wanted Jenna to reject them. To tell them they were way out of their league. It wasn't very nice, Keisha knew, but she didn't want her friends hanging out with Jenna every afternoon. She wanted them to hang out with her. *She* was the one who needed them—not Jenna Scott.

"You're early," Mrs. Johnson said as Keisha entered through the shop's heavy wooden door, making the bells that hung just above it jingle. "I thought you, Sarah, and Emily would stop for ice cream at Scoops on the way. I can't believe you came straight—" Mrs. Johnson paused and glanced out at the sidewalk. "Where are Sarah and Emily? I thought they were coming with you today."

"They both had to go home and clean their rooms," Keisha lied. She didn't feel like explaining to her mother that her friends had ditched her for someone cooler.

Mrs. Johnson narrowed her eyes and stared at Keisha. "I see," she said after a moment. "Well, I'm still surprised you didn't stop for ice cream."

Keisha shrugged. "I don't feel like ice cream today."

"That's good, because you don't look like ice cream, either," Mrs. Johnson said.

Keisha rolled her eyes and walked toward the back of the store where all of the furniture was kept. She ran her hand along the back of an old velvet sofa and then onto the top of a matching wingback chair. Her mom's thrift shop, Something Old, Something New, had some pretty cool stuff—everything from old jewelry and clothes to antique furnishings and lighting fixtures—but somehow it always seemed cooler to Keisha when Sarah and Emily were there to rummage through things with her.

"Is this new?" she asked, picking up a ceramic table lamp with a beaded shade.

"Mm-hm," Mrs. Johnson said. "An antique dealer down the street is going out of business, so I bought up some of his old stock. He had a lot of nice books, which reminds me—the shelves need dusting. Do you think you could take care of that while I run out and get the mail?"

"Sure," Keisha replied. She was used to helping out at her mom's store in the afternoons, and dusting was actually one of her favorite jobs. She loved the bright blue feather duster her mother kept behind the register. When she was younger, she used to play with it, singing into it like it was a microphone or just walking around the store tapping things with it as if it were a magic wand. It had always seemed more like a toy than any kind of cleaning implement to her, which made dusting seem like more of a game than a chore. She still thought it was pretty fun.

"Thanks. I'll be right back," Mrs. Johnson said. She scooped up a few envelopes and started for the door, but she turned around just before she reached it. "Are you sure you don't want ice cream? I could pick something up for you on my way back."

Keisha forced a half smile. She knew she had to look really dejected if her mother, Jackie How-About-a-Healthy-Snack Johnson, was offering ice cream. "Thanks, but I'm not hungry."

"You're turning down ice cream?" Mrs. Johnson said, her eyes wide. "Are you feeling okay?"

"You're offering ice cream. Are *you* feeling okay?" Keisha replied.

Mrs. Johnson smiled. "Touché," she said with a chuckle. "All right. I'll grab the mail and be right back. You hold down the fort."

"Got it," Keisha said. She heard the bells above the door jingle as her mom left, and she went to the register to get the feather duster and some spray. The bookshelves were in the back left corner of the store. They seemed kind of out of the way, but Keisha's mom had explained that she kept them there because books were one of her most popular items. Having them in the back corner of the store meant that people had to walk past a lot of the other merchandise to get to them, increasing the odds that they'd see something else they liked and walk out with more than a book.

Keisha had thought her mother was a genius for coming up with this strategy until her mom had explained that she learned it from the grocery store. "Milk," she had said, "is almost always the farthest away from the door even though it's the thing people buy most. They make you walk past the bread, the candy, the cleaning supplies, *everything* to get to it, and it works. I go in for milk and come out with three bags of groceries."

It made sense. The books were Keisha's favorite part of the store, but on the way back to look at them, she almost always discovered some other treasure that piqued her curiosity. But not today. Today she was too preoccupied with Sarah and Emily and how much fun they were probably having over at Jenna's house. Without her.

She spritzed the end of the feather duster with a little water to moisten it and ran it over the shelves. The water kept the dust from simply flying into the air and resettling somewhere else, and all Keisha had to do was vacuum off the duster once it was dry. It was a trick her mother had taught her—one of many.

Keisha continued to dust the shelves, giving the spines of the books a few strokes here and there as she went. She had just reached the end of the second row of bookcases when she realized she must have found the new books her mother was talking about. There were several faded red hardcovers with dull gold writing that was obviously pretty old. Keisha didn't remember seeing any of them before. *A Room of One's Own, Wuthering Heights, Pride and Prejudice.* There were about fifty books altogether, all with the same faded red covers and gold lettering— except for one. At the end of the collection, there was a much larger book. Its spine stuck out over the edge of the bookshelf, and its cover, while just as faded as the others, was blue. It, too, had distinctive gold lettering, though it was in a fancier cursive script and not quite as faded.

"*Faerie Tales,*" Keisha read, setting down the duster and pulling the book off the shelf. Carefully, she opened the cover and flipped through a few of the thick, glossy pages. Vibrant illustrations with intricate details offset the text. The words in the book were written in big black script that looked like some kind of old-fashioned calligraphy. It was the most beautiful book Keisha had ever seen. All thoughts of dusting left her mind as she sat down in the middle of the aisle to read.

Ten minutes later when her mother returned, she was still reading, and she was so engrossed that she didn't even hear the bells above the door jingle.

"Keisha?"

Keisha jumped, startled by her mother's interruption.

"Where are you?"

"I'm back here," Keisha replied. She'd been reading one of the stories. It was about an Egyptian girl who chose to run away from her village rather than get married. The girl wanted to become a doctor, but her parents and everyone else in her village kept telling her that was an unrealistic dream for a girl in her social class. Instead, they expected her to follow tradition and become a wife and mother before her next birthday.

Unfortunately, Keisha wasn't able to find out how the story ended. The last two pages of the tale had been ripped out, so she was left wondering what became of the poor girl.

"What are you doing?" Mrs. Johnson asked. She had come to find Keisha and was now standing at the end of the aisle, looking down at her. "Is that one of the new books?"

"Mm-hm," Keisha replied without looking up.

"Looks like a nice one," her mother commented.

"It is," Keisha agreed.

Mrs. Johnson watched her daughter as she ran a hand over one of the pictures. "You can bring it home if you want. It doesn't really fit with the rest of the collection anyway."

"Okay," Keisha said absently. She was glad her mother was going to let her take the book, but she was too fascinated with the picture to give a real response. The page she was on had an illustration of the young Egyptian girl floating down a river on a raft. There were crocodiles on either side of her baring their teeth, but she didn't seem to notice them. Instead, she was staring straight forward at the long blue river, with a somber expression on her face.

"Did you hear me, Keisha?" Mrs. Johnson said. "You got a package in the mail."

The word *package* snapped Keisha out of her daze. "I got what?" she asked.

"A package—a small one—and a letter. From Jasmine."

Keisha's eyes widened. Jasmine Porter had been one of her best friends until she'd moved to New Hampshire at the end of their fifth-grade year. Keisha and Jasmine still kept in touch via e-mail and letters, but this was the first time Jasmine had sent a package.

Keisha jumped to her feet, nestling the book under her arm, and followed her mother to the front of the store.

"Here it is," Mrs. Johnson said.

Keisha tore into the envelope on top and removed a small square of paper.

Hey, Keisha—

I got your e-mail the other night. It's too bad you're not in the same home-room as Sarah and Emily, and I'm really sorry you got Mrs. MacKnight. She sounds horrible!

Anyway, you sounded really down in your e-mail, so I thought I'd send some-thing along to help you out. I hope it brings you some good luck.

Your friend forever,
Jasmine

"Hm," Keisha muttered, puzzled by the note. What could it be? She ripped the tape off of the small box to which the note was attached and opened one end, then tilted it up. Out dropped a silver chain. Keisha held it up—a charm bracelet.

"Wow, that's pretty," Mrs. Johnson said as Keisha turned it over in her hand. There were four charms on the bracelet already—an angel, a unicorn, a fairy, and a princess—along with a few turquoise beads and silver hearts.

"She said it's supposed to bring me good luck," Keisha said, still staring at the bracelet.

"That was nice of Jasmine," Mrs. Johnson said. "Do you want me to help you put it on?"

"Sure," Keisha replied. She passed the bracelet to her mother and held out her wrist, and Mrs. Johnson fastened the clasp. Keisha turned her wrist from side to side, admiring the way the silver charms gleamed in the sunlight. "It's nice," she said.

"Yes, it is," Mrs. Johnson agreed. Then with a smile she added, "But the real question is . . . Do you feel luckier yet?"

Keisha started to smile, but just at that moment she heard a familiar laugh outside the shop door. She looked out the huge plate-glass window just in time to catch Sarah, Emily, and Jenna Scott walking down the other side of the street with towels draped around their shoulders, their wet hair glistening in the sun. Each of them was holding a fresh ice-cream cone, probably from the shop right around the corner—the one Keisha, Emily, and Sarah always stopped at when they were hanging out at Mrs. Johnson's store.

Keisha watched as the three girls, smiling and laughing, hopped into a green SUV, which no doubt belonged to Jenna's mother, and disappeared from sight. She couldn't help noticing that neither Sarah nor Emily had so much as glanced at Keisha's mother's store.

"Well, do you?" Mrs. Johnson prompted.

Keisha forced the corners of her mouth upward slightly into the best smile she could manage. "A little," she said, not wanting to disappoint her mother. But, in truth, she wasn't feeling lucky at all.

CHAPTER
Two

"Finally," Keisha murmured, setting her pencil down on her desk. "Done." She gathered up the books that were lying around her—language arts, math, science, and history—along with their corresponding spiral-bound notebooks, stacked them up, and set the whole pile on the floor. As she did, the shining silver chain on her wrist caught her eye.

Keisha touched each of the charms again and smiled. Although the bracelet didn't seem to be bringing her any good luck, it was still nice of Jasmine to send it along.

Keisha powered up her old Macintosh computer—the one that had been in her parents' office up until two weeks ago, when they had gotten a new one—and checked her e-mail. There were no new messages. And she hadn't gotten a phone call from Sarah or Emily, either. *Oh, well*, Keisha thought. It was still early. She glanced at her alarm clock. *Nine-thirty*. It was kind of late for a phone call, actually, but it was still possible that one of them would call. Or e-mail. And in the meantime, Keisha could shoot Jasmine a quick note.

To: jazzypdesigns@nh.teletron.com
From: keishaj123@ma.inet.com
Subject: thanks!

Hey, Jasmine—
   I got your package today. Thanks! The bracelet is really cool, and I'm sure it will be lucky. How's NH? Things r ok here. Mrs. MacKnight is still horrible, but I'm dealing.
   Thanks again for the bracelet.

                              TTFN,
                              Keisha

Keisha clicked SEND and then checked for new messages one more time. Nope. Nothing. Maybe both Emily's and Sarah's parents had forbidden them to e-mail, instant message, or make phone calls until they finished their homework or something.

Keisha shut down the computer with a sigh. She grabbed the book of fairy tales off the desk and flopped down on her bed with it.

Slowly, she flipped through the glossy pages, stopping once again at the picture of the Egyptian girl that had so captivated her in her mother's store. Keisha studied it closely. It looked incredibly lifelike. The cloth of the girl's white tunic actually appeared to be blowing with the breeze, and the brightly colored clay beads of her necklace looked as if they would be warm to the touch.

In her spare time, Keisha loved to paint and draw, and Sarah, Emily, and Jasmine had always told her she was a really good artist. Still, she knew she had never even come close to drawing a person as realistic as the girl in this picture.

There was something about her hair, black, shiny, and straight. And her eyes, deep brown and outlined in kohl. They looked so . . . *real.* And the sadness in her eyes—Keisha could almost feel it. But then, that was probably because she was feeling so alone herself. "I know how you feel," she whispered to the girl, reaching forward to touch the picture. As she did, the bracelet that Jasmine had sent her brushed the page.

What happened next was a blur to Keisha. There was a blinding flash, as though fifty people had taken a picture at the same time, all of them with their flashbulbs pointed directly into Keisha's eyes. "Whoa!" Keisha exclaimed, blinking rapidly. "What was *that!?*" When the spots had finally cleared from her vision, she glanced around the room. Everything still looked the same, and everything still sounded the same. What was going on?

Keisha squinted and rubbed her eyes. "That," she mumbled to herself, "was weird." She glanced around the room, trying to figure out what had just happened, but was unable to come up with any possible explanation. She wondered if she'd imagined the whole thing. Then she looked back down at the book of fairy tales. She gasped.

"Ohmigosh—she's gone!" she cried.

Keisha flipped the pages forward and backward, coming back again and again to the picture of the raft on the river with the crocodiles at its sides. But now the raft was empty. And no matter how many times she did it, she couldn't seem to find the young girl with the dark hair. Somehow, she had completely disappeared.

"I must be losing my mind," Keisha muttered.

"Perhaps I could help you to find it," a small voice replied.

Keisha jumped backward on her bed. "Who said that?" she gasped.

"I did," the small voice replied.

Keisha scanned her room to find the source of the voice, but it wasn't until she felt a tiny tickle on her left toe that she found it. There, balanced on the tip of her slipper, was the girl from the fairy tale book. She was only about two inches tall, but she was there nonetheless. Her black hair reflected the light from Keisha's desk lamp, and her dark eyes, which had appeared so sad in the picture, now shone with excitement. Her tiny tunic was bright white.

"How—? What—?" Keisha stammered.

"I beg your pardon," the small girl said, bowing low. "I did not mean to startle you." She looked around Keisha's room, taking in the yellow walls, the hardwood floor, and Keisha's red throw rug. "If you do not mind my asking, what is this place?"

Keisha stared at the small Egyptian. *I'm dreaming*, she thought. *I must be dreaming.* She grasped the flesh of her upper arm between her thumb and forefinger and pinched it as hard as she could. "Ouch!"

"Are you all right?" the small girl asked, scurrying down Keisha's flexed foot toward her ankle. Her footsteps were so light and feathery that they tickled Keisha. Keisha jumped, sending the small girl flying into the air. She flew through the air and landed facedown on Keisha's bed.

"Oh, no—I'm sorry," Keisha sputtered. "I didn't mean to . . . I mean, are you okay?" Slowly, she leaned nearer to the small being, her mind whirling. She was nervous to be so close to the tiny figure, yet worried that she had hurt it, and still a bit afraid that none of this was real and that she truly had lost her mind.

The Egyptian girl raised herself onto her knees and brushed herself off, straightened her tunic, adjusted her belt, and moved her necklace so that it hung properly. "I seem to be fine," she said. She raised her gaze and met Keisha's eyes. "Are *you* all right?"

"I'm—" Keisha started. "Well, yeah. I guess I am. I'm just . . . confused. You were in the book and then . . . *how did you get here?*"

"I am not certain," the girl replied. "One

moment I was drifting down the river, searching for a new home, and the next moment I found myself here, in this strange new world."

"But you're not real. I mean, you came out of a book. You can't be real." Keisha pressed her eyes closed, then opened them again, half-expecting the small figure to be gone, but she wasn't. "I have to be imagining this."

The small girl shook her head. "I assure you that I am quite real. How I came to be here, I cannot explain, but I am no more a part of your imagination than you are a part of mine."

Keisha rubbed her eyes as she listened to the girl's words. She'd read stories about characters popping out of books, and dolls coming to life, but she'd never heard about anything like that happening in the real world. And yet, here was the girl from the picture standing right in front of her. "Hold on a second," she said.

Quickly—and quietly—Keisha ran over to her bedroom door, closed it, and turned the lock. "No offense," she added, glancing at the small figure on her bed. "I just don't really want anyone to catch me sitting here talking to you. You know, like if you're not really . . . *real*."

The girl smiled. "I understand your concern,"

she said. "But I promise you I am as real as you are."

"Yeah, well, even if you are, I'm not sure I want to have to explain you to my parents." Keisha cocked her head to one side, imagining the conversation. *Hey, Mom, Dad, remember that book I brought home from the store today? Yeah, well, one of the characters came to life and she's hanging out in my room. Wanna meet her?* Something told her that wouldn't go over too well.

The tiny girl gave a slight laugh. "I understand your predicament," she said. "My parents would have difficulty believing me if I told them that I had sailed to a land of giants."

Keisha scowled. "I'm not a giant," she said. "Giants are big, ugly things that eat people and stuff."

The girl's dark eyes grew wide with concern. "Forgive me," she replied. "I didn't mean to insult you. I just assumed . . . well, you are so much larger than I am—I thought—"

"It's okay," Keisha said with a shrug. "I'm like, fifty times your size. I guess I am a giant to you."

"And I must be like a scarab to you," the girl replied.

Keisha walked back to her bed and slowly,

carefully, so as not to jostle her guest, lay down facing the small girl. She propped her head up on her elbows and for a moment she just stared, taking in every last detail of the tiny figure in front of her. It was amazing. The girl looked just like she did in the book—shiny dark hair, large brown eyes, white ankle-length tunic, bare feet. She seemed even more beautiful and delicate now that she existed in three dimensions.

"You are pretty small," she said. "I'm really sorry I sent you flying before. Are you okay?"

"Yes, indeed," the girl replied. "Your pallet is most comfortable."

"My *pallet*?"

"Yes. This platform we are on. I assume it is where you take your rest."

"Oh, my *bed*," Keisha said.

"Yes, your bed," the girl repeated. "It is so soft. It is as though it has been lined with the feathers of the Great Gray Heron."

Keisha laughed. "That's because of my comforter," she said. "It is full of feathers, but not from the Great Gray Heron. More like the small gray goose. It's stuffed with down."

"Goose feathers," the girl murmured. Then she stood up, stretched herself tall, and fell backward with her arms extended. "Ahh," she said once she had landed on her back. "It is quite pleasing. I must tell my mother—" She stopped short, covering her mouth with one hand. "Oh, my, I almost forgot," she said slowly. "I shall not be seeing my mother again in this lifetime."

The girl's eyes clouded over then, and the sparkle of excitement was gone. Once more she appeared as despondent as she had seemed in the illustration.

"Why not?" Keisha asked.

"I had to leave my village," the girl replied simply, her voice slow and sad, "and I can never return."

Keisha leaned farther forward, so concerned with the reason for the tiny girl's distress that she had forgotten to wonder whether or not she was real. "Why? What happened?"

With a snort, the girl sat upright and folded her arms across her chest. "It is not what happened," she said. "It is what would have happened if I had stayed."

Keisha stared, wide-eyed, waiting for her tiny visitor to continue, but the girl remained silent, her eyes narrowed and her lips pursed. "*What*?" Keisha prompted. "What was so bad that you had to run away?"

The girl looked up at Keisha, still scowling. "Marriage," she replied flatly.

"Oh, right," Keisha said, glancing back at the book of fairy tales. "That's what it said in the story. But I don't get it. Why would you be getting married? I mean, how old are you, anyway?"

"I am sixteen," the girl replied. "But most girls in my village are married by the age of fourteen."

Keisha gasped. "Ohmigosh! That's only eighth grade."

The small girl furrowed her brow. "What is *eighth grade*? Is this how your people measure age?"

"Huh? Oh, no," Keisha said, shaking her head. "Eighth grade is just a year in school. See, we—"

"You attend school?" The girl opened her eyes so wide that her long, dark eyelashes nearly touched her eyebrows. "That is my dream! You must take me with you."

"To *school*?" Keisha asked.

"Yes. I wish to become a physician, but only members of higher classes may study at the House of Life."

"The *House of Life*?"

"Yes, it is a part of the temple where sacred texts are kept. People go there to study mathematics, science, reading, writing, and sometimes medicine. But," the girl said sadly, "it is not open to everyone."

"Wow. It didn't say anything about that in here," Keisha said, picking up the book. "Maybe it would have, though, if these pages weren't missing."

Keisha held the book in her lap, and the small girl jumped onto the page with the picture of the raft and the crocodiles.

"This is where I came from?" the small girl asked.

Keisha nodded. "Mm-hm. You were in that picture."

The girl stared down at the raft in the clear blue river. "Yes," she said, nodding. "I remember." She hopped onto the left-hand page, which was filled with text, and began scanning it. "And this is my story. But you say there are pages missing?"

"The last two," Keisha said. "But *you* must know how it ends."

The tiny figure shook her head. "I only know that I have been drifting on that river for many, many moons." She gazed over at the picture. For a moment, Keisha thought the girl was going to cry, but then she brightened. "But perhaps the pages are missing because the rest of my story does not take place in the book. Perhaps my story ends here, in your world."

Keisha lowered one eyebrow. She had a hard time believing that this two-inch-tall ancient Egyptian character was meant to live out the rest of her life in the twenty-first century.

"Tell me," the girl said, her eyes gleaming. "What do they teach at your school?"

Keisha thought about Mrs. MacKnight's obsession with correct posture and her constant reviews of the school rules. "*Not* medicine," she started, "but—"

"Are you able to read?"

Keisha blinked, confused. "Of course I can read. I'm almost twelve and I've been reading since I was five." She eyed her small Egyptian friend. "Can *you*?"

"Yes," the girl answered. "And I can write, too, but only because I taught myself. Very few people in my village ever learn. Neither of my parents can read or write. It is not considered important in our lives."

"Wow," Keisha said. She tried to imagine what it would be like to live without books and stories and poems, without magazines and newspapers, without signs and instruction manuals. She couldn't. And yet this girl had grown up with none of it. "But wait—if no one around you could read or write, how did you learn?"

"With the help of my friend Siamun," the girl replied. "His father is a scribe, so he learned when he was very young."

"And he taught you?"

"Yes," the girl said with a broad grin. "Siamun is very intelligent. He has been a great friend to me. I miss him terribly." As she spoke, the girl stared up at Keisha's ceiling, and for a moment she seemed to be a million miles away. Or maybe just a couple of thousand years.

"Is Siamun the guy you were supposed to marry?" Keisha asked.

The little Egyptian gasped. "Siamun?" she exclaimed. Then she closed her eyes and shook her head. "No. Siamun is a scribe. I could never hope to marry him."

"But . . . it seems like you really like him," Keisha protested.

The girl nodded. "I do," she said. "But my father is a farmer. If I were to marry, it would be to a peasant—not to someone of a higher social class."

"Siamun's from a higher class?"

"Yes. Farmers, like my father, are part of the

lowest class. Scribes are much higher, and people do not often marry outside of their own class."

"Why not?" Keisha asked.

The girl shrugged. "To keep order, I suppose. I am not certain. I only know that it is not done."

Keisha clicked her tongue. "That stinks. So you can't marry Siamun or study to be a doctor just because your father's a farmer?"

"That is correct."

"Well . . . what *can* you do? I mean, it sounds like you're kind of stuck."

The girl frowned. "It is true. I do not have many options. I had hoped that by learning to read and write, I could gain admittance to the House of Life. Sometimes people can rise from their social class through education, but it is difficult—especially for girls. We are expected to marry so young, and once married we must have children and take care of our homes. That is fine for many women. My mother is very happy. But *I* want to be a physician."

"So you ran away."

"Yes. And now I am here," the girl said.

"Wow," Keisha replied, shaking her head. "And I thought I had problems just because my friends ditched me after school."

"Your friends put you in a ditch?" the small girl exclaimed.

"What? Oh—no," Keisha laughed. "They didn't put me *in* a ditch. They ditched me. It means they blew me off." The small girl furrowed her brow. "It's like . . . deciding not to hang out with someone because you got a better offer."

"Hang out?" the girl questioned.

Keisha wrinkled her nose. "I'm not explaining this very well, am I?" she said. "Okay, so *hang out* means spend time with someone, and getting a better offer is like having something more fun to do. So my friends were supposed to spend time with me, but they found something better to do. Does that make sense?"

"I think so," the girl replied. "But if they found something better to do, why did you not go with them?" she asked.

Keisha bit her lip. "That's the whole point," she said. "They didn't invite me. See, we were supposed to go see a movie—I'll explain what that is later—but then my friends decided they'd rather hang out with someone else. *Without me*."

"Ohhh," the girl said, nodding her head. "I see. And that is called blowing off?"

Keisha squinted. "Sort of," she said. "But you don't just blow off—you blow some*thing* off. Like when you're supposed to do something but then you decide not to, you say you blew it off."

"I see." The girl nodded again, but Keisha could tell from the creases on the little Egyptian's forehead that she was still a bit confused. "You use many unique expressions. I wish I could understand them better."

"I can help you with that," Keisha offered.

"That would be wonderful. And perhaps I shall learn some more at your school as well."

"Right, school," Keisha said. "About that . . ." She was trying to think of a way to explain to the little Egyptian that it was going to be kind of difficult for her just to show up at Adams Middle School. For one thing, she wasn't registered. And for another, she was only two inches tall.

"When shall we go?" the girl asked.

"Well, I have school tomorrow," Keisha hedged, "but—"

"Good. I shall accompany you. But first I shall take some rest. My journey has made me quite weary."

With that, the girl lay down at the foot of Keisha's bed. She placed her hands together beneath her head for a pillow and closed her eyes.

Keisha watched her for a moment, baffled as to what to do or say. "Um, hey," she called, but the girl's eyes remained closed. "Hello?" Keisha called, gently prodding one of her guest's tiny feet.

The girl opened her eyes and sat up. "Yes?"

"I just realized—I don't even know your name."

"Oh! Forgive me," the girl said, standing up and facing Keisha. She brought her palms together in front of her chest and executed a small bow. "I am Naeemah, daughter of Ammun and Dalila in the village of Akhenaten."

"Naeemah," Keisha said. "I like that name. It's pretty."

The tiny girl smiled and bowed again, then looked expectantly at Keisha.

"Oh," Keisha said. She stood up and brought her hands together, imitating Naeemah's gesture. "Um, I'm Keisha, daughter of Roger and Jackie in the city of Boston." She bowed, then straightened up abruptly.

"I am pleased to make your acquaintance, Keisha, and I thank you for sharing your chamber with me."

"No problem," Keisha said. Naeemah gave her a sideways glance. "That means I'm happy to—it's *not* a problem," Keisha added quickly.

Naeemah smiled. "Thank you," she said. "I look forward to furthering my education with you tomorrow."

"Yeah, about that—" Keisha started again, but Naeemah was already lying down, making herself comfortable, and within seconds she appeared to be asleep.

"Naeemah?" Keisha whispered, but her little friend didn't stir at all. "I guess jumping out of storybooks makes you pretty tired," Keisha mumbled to herself. She walked over to her bureau and grabbed a blue bandanna that was lying on top of it. Folding it into a square, she took it back to the bed and draped it over Naeemah like a little blanket.

For a few minutes, Keisha sat on the edge of her bed watching Naeemah sleep, her tiny chest rising and falling with each breath. How, and why, had this tiny girl from ancient Egypt come to be in her room?

Keisha was no longer wondering whether or not Naeemah was real—Keisha was positive she was. But what Keisha really needed to figure out was what she was going to do with

Naeemah now that she was here, and how she was going to smuggle her into school tomorrow. Mrs. MacKnight didn't even allow gum in class. What was she going to say about a two-inch-tall ancient Egyptian?

CHAPTER
Three

"I'm still not sure why you want to come to school with me," Keisha said to Naeemah, who was standing in her palm. They were standing on the sidewalk outside of Keisha's house, waiting for the bus to come.

"I seek knowledge," Naeemah answered matter-of-factly.

"Yeah," Keisha replied, "I know. But I'm not sure you're going to find the kind of knowledge you're looking for at Adams. I mean, sometimes we do cool things, but we don't read a lot of . . . doctor stuff."

Naeemah gazed into Keisha's eyes, her own dark irises gleaming. "I shall be pleased with any knowledge I can obtain," she said. "In my culture, girls do not traditionally receive an education outside the home. It is a privilege for me to attend your school." As was her habit, the tiny girl bowed low to Keisha once again.

"You don't have to do that, you know," Keisha said. "It makes me feel like you're my servant or something."

Naeemah stood up straight. "I apologize," she said, bowing.

"You just did it again."

"Oh, my, I am terribly sorry," Naeemah said—with another bow.

"And again!" Keisha said, pointing at Naeemah with her free hand. "Wow! Hard habit to break, huh?"

"I am having difficulty stopping, yes," Naeemah replied. She brought her arms to her sides and stood rigidly. She held herself in this awkward posture for a few seconds before suddenly jumping up and down and pointing. "Look!" she yelled excitedly. "Here comes the . . . the . . . the . . . bacon!"

"The *bacon*?" Keisha repeated. She turned and looked over her shoulder, then glanced back at Naeemah. "Okay, I know we went over a lot this morning," she said, referring to the crash course she'd given Naeemah earlier in stuff-we-might-see-on-the-way-to-school, "but bacon is that crispy, meaty stuff we ate at breakfast. *That*," she continued, pointing down the road, "is the *bus*."

"Ah, yes, the bus," Naeemah said, blushing slightly. "I knew it started with a B."

Keisha laughed. "Yeah, you were close," she said. She held open the pocket of her windbreaker and nodded to her little friend. "Why don't you hop in here while we get on the bus. It'll be easier for me to carry you that way. And stay out of sight, too. I don't want anyone to see you and start asking questions."

"Why not?" Naeemah asked.

"Because you're different," Keisha asked. "If people find out about you, they'll want to take you away and bring you to a lab and put you in a box and study you for science or something."

Naeemah jumped into Keisha's windbreaker, disappearing for a moment before she poked her head back out. "I do not think I would like that at all," she said.

"That's why you should stay hidden," Keisha replied, pushing Naeemah's head back down into her pocket as the big yellow school bus stopped in front of her. She waited for the folding door to open, then climbed up the steep stairs and made her way to her seat.

As she approached, she saw Emily and Sarah, who sat directly behind her, whispering and laughing, which made her feel a bit self-conscious. *It's not about me, it's not about me,* she told herself, but she wasn't entirely convinced. After seeing them outside her mother's shop yesterday acting so chummy with the amazing Jenna Scott, Keisha couldn't help feeling a little insecure. Still, she managed to smile and act natural as she sat down.

"Hey, guys, what's up?" she asked, tucking one leg underneath herself so she could face backward in her seat. "Did you have fun at Jenna's?"

"The best," Emily said. "Her house is so cool, and her swimming pool is awesome!"

"It's Olympic size," Sarah added, "and it's heated."

"Yeah. I know," Keisha replied.

Emily narrowed her eyes. "How do *you* know?"

"You told me yesterday," Keisha replied. "Remember?"

"Oh. Right," Emily said.

"Hey, Keisha, you should come to the movies with us this weekend," Sarah said. "It'll be cool."

"Why would you want to go if it will be cold?" a small voice said in Keisha's ear.

Keisha turned her head to see that Naeemah

had somehow managed to climb out of her pocket and up her sleeve to her shoulder. Keisha jumped slightly and emitted a mild scream, causing Naeemah to wobble and her friends to stare. "I . . . I thought that car was going to run into us," she improvised, pointing toward the back window.

Emily and Sarah turned around, giving Keisha a chance to scowl at Naeemah.

"I know I was supposed to stay in your pocket, but they do not seem able to see or hear me," Naeemah stated calmly. Sure enough, when Emily and Sarah turned back around, they showed no indication that they were aware of the two-inch-tall figure perched on Keisha's shoulder.

"So what do you say, Keish? Do you want to come to the movies this weekend?" Emily asked, nudging Sarah.

Keisha pressed her lips together. Why was Emily smirking at her like that?

"I don't know. Is *Fly Girl II* still playing?" Keisha asked.

"Yep," Emily replied, swishing her long brown hair over her shoulder. "But we're not going for the movie." Emily glanced sideways at Sarah.

Keisha wrinkled her nose. "What do you mean?" she asked.

"She means that Noah Carpenter is going to be there," Sarah said with a mischievous grin.

Keisha narrowed her eyes. "So?"

"Are you kidding?" Sarah and Emily said at the same time.

"Noah Carpenter is the cutest guy in our class," Emily said.

Keisha felt a tug on one of the wispy hairs just behind her ear. "Does that mean he is a good marriage match?" Naeemah asked.

"No," Keisha replied. Then, realizing her friends were staring at her, she added, "I mean, I don't think he's all that cute."

Both Sarah's and Emily's eyes nearly popped out of their heads.

"Are you serious?" Sarah asked.

"Have you looked at him lately?" Emily added.

"I don't know," Keisha said. If she had, what was she supposed to notice? Even if he was cute, as Sarah and Emily kept insisting, that didn't mean that Keisha would want to hang around with him. "I guess it's just that I've known him since nursery school," Keisha went on, "when he used to sit in the sandbox eating the sand, remember? And I don't know, I just don't think he's very nice. He's always making fun of people and stuff."

Emily and Sarah looked stricken.

"He's just being *funny*, Keish. Geez," Emily said. "Have a sense of humor."

"I do," Keisha said. "I just don't like it when people make fun of other people."

"That is very honorable of you," Naeemah said. "In my culture, respect for one's peers and elders is very important."

That's great, Keisha thought. *Maybe I should try moving to ancient Egypt.*

"Well, you don't have to like Noah—he's Jenna's, anyway," Emily said.

"They're practically a couple," Sarah added.

"Yeah," Emily continued, "and Jenna wants to sit with him, so she needs us there to make sure the other guys don't just hang around and bother them the whole time."

"The other guys?" Keisha asked.

"You know, Justin Chapman, Luke Davidson— the usual crowd."

"Oh, and Noah's little brother," Sarah added. "Seth."

"Oh, that's right," Emily said. "Jenna was wondering if you could sit with him, Keisha. We told her you might want to come, and she said you'd be perfect for Seth."

Naeemah clapped her hands. "How wonderful!

They're including you this time instead of blow-ing you up," she said.

Keisha heard her pint-size friend's mistake, but she was too annoyed to correct her. "*Seth Carpenter?*" she said.

Emily nodded. "I'm sitting with Justin, and Sarah's sitting with Luke, so we thought you could sit with Seth."

"But he's a fourth grader!" Keisha objected.

"Yeah, but he's Noah's brother," Sarah said, as if that were some consolation.

"I don't care. I'm not going to the movies with him," Keisha said.

Emily rolled her eyes and exhaled heavily. "Come on, Keisha," she said in a frustrated tone. "I mean, it's not like you're into anyone else. Why can't you just come to the movies and sit with Seth?"

Keisha narrowed her eyes. Over the summer, Emily and Sarah had both started crushing on boys at their school and had started calling and instant messaging them all the time. But Keisha hadn't. She didn't mind hanging out with boys or anything, but she wasn't really interested in dating them or even flirting a lot. And she defi-nitely didn't think any of the boys at Adams Middle School were hotties.

All summer, Emily and Sarah knew how she felt and they'd been fine with it. The three of them had still been able to hang out and have fun together, and neither Emily nor Sarah had ever given Keisha a hard time. Until now.

"Because I'm not a babysitter!" Keisha fired back.

Emily folded her arms across her chest and sneered at Keisha. "No, you're just a *baby*!" Sarah clapped her hand to her mouth, but not before a laugh had escaped.

Naeemah stood up on Keisha's shoulder, her hands on her hips. "That was unkind. You are not a baby," she told Keisha firmly. "That girl is the one who whines like an infant!" She pointed at Emily.

Suddenly, all the chatter on the bus was interrupted by a high-pitched screeching sound. Everyone whirled toward Emily to see her sitting with her head thrown back, shrieking like a hysterical newborn.

Sarah's mouth was hanging open in shock. And Emily, once she had stopped screaming, pulled her shoulders up to her ears and wrapped her arms around herself, her olive skin eight shades of red.

"What was that?" Kristen Carmichael, a

popular eighth grader, asked from three rows back. Emily covered her face with her hands, and Sarah began to shrink down in her seat.

While Sarah and Emily were busy making themselves as small as possible, Keisha covered her mouth to hide her amusement and turned around, facing the front of the bus.

"Why did you do that?" she heard Sarah ask, to which Emily responded with a burbling noise. "Stop it," Sarah hissed. "Everyone's looking at us."

Good, Keisha thought. They deserved a little humiliation for what they'd been trying to do. So she didn't have a crush on anybody. That didn't mean they had to pawn her off on some fourth grader. They were supposed to want her around because she was their friend—not to occupy some kid.

When she had managed to stifle her indignation, and her giggles, Keisha turned to Naeemah. "Did you make her cry like that?"

Naeemah winced. "I believe I did," she said gravely. "I am very sorry. I—"

"Don't worry about it," Keisha said. "I'm not mad at you or anything. She totally deserved it. I think you did the right—"

"That is not the problem," Naeemah interrupted.

Keisha narrowed her eyes. "What do you mean?"

Naeemah gazed up at her, her brown eyes wider than ever. "I am not a magician. I have never made anything like that happen before, and I was not trying to."

"You mean, that was an accident?" Keisha asked. Naeemah nodded. "But how could—?"

"I do not know," Naeemah replied, and the two of them exchanged a nervous glance. Not only had Naeemah emerged from a storybook without either of them understanding how, but now it seemed that she had acquired some sort of magical power along the way—a power that she had no idea how to use.

CHAPTER
Four

"As I explained yesterday," Mrs. MacKnight droned, "the civilization of the Mycenae in Greece was one of the most accomplished town-building civilizations in ancient times." She'd been lecturing on ancient European civilizations for nearly thirty minutes now, and Keisha was about ready to fall asleep.

To keep herself occupied, Keisha was sketching a picture of Naeemah, who was sitting on an eraser at the corner of Keisha's desk with her hands neatly folded on her lap.

"This map shows the boundaries of ancient Greece and the various peoples who inhabited it." Mrs. MacKnight tapped a pull-down map that covered part of the chalkboard. "If you'll look closely," she went on, but Keisha ignored her. She was more intent on getting Naeemah's nose right. It was angular, but not too pointed, and Keisha wanted to get the lines perfect.

"If I may inquire, what is the duration of this particular lesson?" Naeemah asked, turning to face Keisha.

"Huh?" Keisha muttered.

Naeemah sighed. It was the first time Keisha had noticed her looking frustrated since she had arrived. "How long will we be listening to this woman?" Naeemah said.

Keisha chuckled. "Boring, isn't it?" She hunched over so that no one could see her lips moving.

"Posture, Miss Johnson," Mrs. MacKnight suddenly barked.

Keisha sat up straight.

"That's better," Mrs. MacKnight said. "Now, do you have something you'd like to share with the class?"

"Uh, no," Keisha ventured. If she'd wanted to share anything with the class, she would have raised her hand, not muttered something under her breath.

Mrs. MacKnight tilted her head and stared directly into Keisha's eyes. "Oh. I thought I heard you whispering, but I must have been wrong. My mistake."

Phew, Keisha thought. *That was close.*

"I have noticed, however, that you've been taking steady notes throughout the class," Mrs. MacKnight went on. "Do you mind if I have a look at them?" Before Keisha could respond, Mrs. MacKnight took her notebook from her desk and examined Keisha's sketch of Naeemah.

"It's wonderful that you are so fond of drawing," she said, holding the picture up for the rest of the class to see. A few students smiled and one or two even gave a small snort, but no one dared to laugh outright. Mrs. MacKnight detested outbursts. "Unfortunately, this is not the art room, and we are not studying ancient Egypt, Miss Johnson." She returned the notebook to Keisha's desk and flipped to a fresh page. "Please keep your mind—and your pencil—on the subject at hand," she said, tapping the paper in front of Keisha.

Keisha swallowed hard. "Yes, ma'am."

Naeemah stared at Mrs. MacKnight. "Is this what all of your teachers are like?" she asked.

Not wishing to draw attention to herself by whispering again, Keisha wrote in the notebook for Naeemah to see: *No, just MacKnight. She's lame.*

"She is lame?" Naeemah asked, pointing at the teacher.

At that moment, Mrs. MacKnight started toward the back of the room to continue her lecture, but she didn't get very far. With her next step, her knee buckled and she went tumbling to the floor. There were a few gasps, and then everyone in the room froze.

Keisha stared at Naeemah, and Naeemah, her hand clasped over her mouth, stared back. Keisha raised her eyebrows at her little friend, and Naeemah slowly nodded. "Yes, I believe I may have done that, too," she said.

"Miss Johnson," Mrs. MacKnight said when she had gotten to her feet. "Tripping your teacher is simply not acceptable. I will see you in my room this afternoon for detention."

"But I didn't—" Keisha started.

"No buts," Mrs. MacKnight said. "Two-thirty P.M., right here." She then cleared her throat and continued walking to the rear of the room.

Keisha brought her hands to her face, exhaled heavily. Detention. She'd never had one before, but she knew enough about Mrs. MacKnight's detentions to know that they lasted at least an hour, no matter what you were there for. And if Mrs. MacKnight really believed that Keisha had tripped her, she was bound to be there for a long time.

That meant she would miss her bus, and her mother would have to come pick her up. *On a day when I'm supposed to be helping out in the store. Oh, man,* Keisha thought. Her mother would have to close down to come get her. She was not going to be pleased.

When Mrs. MacKnight was in the far corner of the room, Keisha dared another look at Naeemah, then she scribbled another note on the back of her picture. *Detention = hanging out with MacKnight after school.*

Naeemah read it and winced. "I am very sorry," she said. "I will try to manage this new strange power more responsibly."

Keisha shrugged. It wasn't Naeemah's fault—at least not really.

Keisha began to take notes on the ancient Greeks. She'd barely written a sentence when a tightly folded square landed on her paper. Keisha glanced to her left and saw Amanda Littlefield smiling at her.

Slowly, Keisha unfolded the note, carefully hiding it in her lap. Inside she found a picture Amanda had drawn that looked like an advertisement in a magazine. MACKNIGHT EX: THE SLEEP AID THAT WORKS IN SECONDS it read across the top. Below, there was a picture of Mrs. MacKnight—Keisha knew it was her from the round glasses and the dark hair pulled back into a bun—standing in front of a room full of people, all slumped over desks, sleeping. Next to Mrs. MacKnight, there was a speech bubble filled with the words BLAH, BLAH, BLAH, repeated over and over again.

Keisha stifled a laugh and refolded the note, dropping it into her backpack. She glanced back at Amanda, but Amanda was sitting up straight, looking directly ahead like the most studious person in the world. That was probably a good idea, Keisha decided. Her mom was going to be angry enough when she found out Keisha had gotten one detention. She'd better make sure she didn't end up with two.

CHAPTER
Five

"I admit that social studies with that awful woman was tedious," Naeemah said from her perch on Keisha's shoulder, "but you must grant me this: Math and art were quite intriguing."

Intriguing? She wasn't sure she'd go that far, but they'd definitely been better than Mrs. MacKnight's class. Almost anything was. She followed along with the rest of the students from Mrs. MacKnight's class as they filed past the office, the library, and the computer lab. Other teachers dismissed their students for lunch, but Mrs. MacKnight insisted upon walking hers to the cafeteria in an orderly fashion so they wouldn't get into trouble.

Keisha had purposely positioned herself at the back of the line today. For one thing, it was easier to whisper to Naeemah back there without being seen or heard. But even more importantly, it was far away from Mrs. MacKnight. And that, Keisha figured, reduced the chances of more accidental magic earning her another detention.

"You are a gifted artist," Naeemah went on, smiling up at Keisha.

"You think so?" Keisha asked out the side of her mouth.

"Certainly. Not only was your sketch of me very lifelike, but the design you created in art class was quite vibrant, too."

Keisha smiled. She did enjoy art class, and Ms. Rainey was a fantastic teacher. Unlike Mrs. MacKnight, she was really personable. She always wore jeans and big white smocks covered with paint, and she always had a smile for everyone.

"Yeah, art is fun, and this is my other favorite class," Keisha murmured as they entered the cafeteria. "Lunch—no boring teachers and no homework."

Once in line, she stood on her toes and craned her neck to see what was written on the menu board. Sometimes the food was kind of gross, like today—fish patties with tartar sauce. Luckily, there were always things like French fries and yogurt that Keisha could buy to get her through the afternoon.

As Keisha pushed her tray along the metal counter, Naeemah watched intently. "These foods are vastly different from those to which I am accustomed. I am eager to try some of this . . . *fish patty*. What kind of fish does it contain?"

"Good question," Keisha replied as she headed for the register. "Let me know if you figure it out."

After paying, she turned around and looked for a place to sit. Emily and Sarah were at one end of a table near the back, but after the way they'd acted that morning, she wasn't sure she wanted to sit with them. Then again, there weren't many other options available, and sitting alone would have made her feel like a loser.

As she made her way to the table, Naeemah jumped down to her tray and stared up at her disapprovingly. "You are going to sit with *them*? After the way they behaved on the . . . large yellow transport."

"The school bus," Keisha said.

"Yes. The school bus," Naeemah agreed. "They were terribly cruel."

Keisha shrugged. "It wasn't *that* bad," she

said, trying to convince herself as well as Naeemah. "Besides, they're my friends." Who else was she going to hang out with?

"Hi, guys," she said, trying to sound upbeat as she set her tray down next to Sarah's.

"That seat's for Jenna," Emily blurted.

Keisha stopped herself short of sitting down. She felt as if she'd been slapped. "Oh. Okay." She stood up and started to slide her tray over one spot, but she was stopped again.

"And that one's for Noah," Sarah said. "Jenna asked him to sit with her at lunch. They're kind of seeing each other now."

"Were they unable to see each other before?" Naeemah asked, confused, but Keisha ignored her. Instead, she tried pushing her tray over to the other side of the table, closer to Emily.

"And since Noah's going to be sitting here, some of his friends are going to want to sit here, too," Emily added. Keisha's mouth dropped open slightly. Since when had she become so unimportant to her friends? Her *best* friends? She was just about ready to give up altogether when Sarah spoke.

"You could sit . . . down there," she suggested, pointing to a space about three stools down from Emily. "Couldn't she, Emily?"

Emily wrinkled her nose. "Well . . ." She counted on her fingers, mouthing names as she did so, and then finally nodded. "Yeah, that should be okay."

Keisha walked around to the seat her friends had indicated. She stood next to it, staring over at Emily and Sarah. As far away from them as she was, she might as well have been at a separate table. It wasn't exactly going to be easy to talk to them from such a distance, but they didn't seem to care.

This is crazy, Keisha thought. Just yesterday the three of them had sat together at lunch and had a good time. Granted, they'd spent a lot of time talking about Jenna—and Noah, and Luke, and Justin, and a bunch of other stuff Keisha didn't really care about, but at least they'd saved her a seat. Now it was like they didn't even want her around. What had happened?

"Are you saving seats like I told you?" Jenna asked, setting her tray next to Sarah's and glancing at Keisha suspiciously.

"Oh, good, *Jenna*," Emily said, as if all of her problems had been solved. "You know Keisha, right?"

Jenna gave Keisha a lukewarm smile. "Sure," she said, then she turned back to Emily and

Sarah. "What's going on?" she asked, sounding a bit irritated.

"We were just trying to figure out where Keisha could sit," Emily said.

"Oh," Jenna said. Keisha squirmed as Jenna eyed her skeptically. She was beginning to feel like an uninvited guest at a private party. "Well, let's see. I'm sitting next to Sarah, and Noah's sitting next to me, then Justin. And on your side, Emmy—"

Keisha gaped at Emily. *Emmy?* she thought. Emily hated it when people shortened her name, or at least she always *used to* hate it.

"You want Luke to sit next to you, right?" Jenna asked.

Emily smiled, blushing slightly. "Yeah."

"Okay, so it will be you, Luke, Justin, and then Keisha can sit on the end. Okay?"

"Okay," Emily said brightly, then she, Sarah, and Jenna all sat down and started gossiping about something that had happened during gym class that morning.

Meanwhile, Keisha remained standing, staring at her friends in disbelief. The boys weren't even here yet, and they wanted her to sit three seats away. She glanced down at Naeemah, who was shaking her head as she watched the three girls. And Naeemah didn't even know the worst of it.

For some reason, Noah Carpenter always seemed to be picking on Keisha, singling her out and making her feel awkward. Keisha's mom always said that was the way boys flirted with girls they liked, but it had never made Keisha feel liked at all. It just made her uncomfortable, and she never knew how to respond. At least in the past, her friends had always stood up for her. But now . . . she wasn't sure she could count on them for much support at all.

"Um, I'm just going to go grab a yogurt," Keisha said, picking up her tray. Neither Emily, Sarah, nor Jenna looked up. They were either too enthralled in their conversation about how cute Noah was when he played soccer, or they didn't care that she was leaving. Keisha didn't want to know which.

"They are insensitive," Naeemah said. She climbed onto Keisha's shoulder and turned around, scowling at Keisha's inconsiderate friends. "They have made you uncomfortable, and they don't even seem to care."

Keisha blinked her eyes, aware that they were beginning to sting with tears.

"They should be made to feel uncomfortable," Naeemah said, pointing at the three girls. "Like donkeys in the heat of summer when the gnats are biting!"

Keisha stopped and stared at her small friend, surprised at the angry outburst. "Isn't that kind of—" She was going to say *harsh*, but she was interrupted by Emily's high-pitched "Ouch!"

Naeemah gasped. "I should not have said that."

"Let's find another table. Quick," Keisha said, speeding up her step. As she and Naeemah rushed away, they could hear the three girls behind them.

"I think something bit me," Emily said.

"I'm so itchy all of a sudden," Jenna added.

"Me, too," Sarah agreed.

"Maybe there's something wrong with this food," Jenna whined.

Keisha sneaked a peek backward to see all three of them madly scratching at their arms, their legs, their necks—everywhere.

"Oops," Naeemah squeaked.

"Oops is right," Keisha agreed.

"I must do something to help them," Naeemah said. "I certainly did not mean to inflict pain on your friends."

Keisha shook her head. "They're not in pain," she said. "They're just itchy and . . . *uncomfortable*, like you said."

"Yes, but—"

"Besides, I'm sure it won't last long. On the bus this morning, Emily got her regular voice back after a minute or two. And Mrs. MacKnight was only lame for a second."

"This is true," Naeemah said. "My magic does not seem to have lasting power."

"Right," Keisha agreed with a small smile. "So don't worry about them—worry about finding us a seat."

"All right," Naeemah said. She turned and sat down on Keisha's shoulder with a sigh. "I will do that."

"Hey, Keisha!"

Surprised to hear someone calling her name, Keisha turned to see Amanda sitting at the end of a table by herself. "Did you make her yell to me?" she asked Naeemah.

"I don't think so," Naeemah said. "But let us take lunch with her. She seems very kind."

Keisha hesitated. Amanda did seem nice, but she had a reputation for being pretty weird. She was always wearing brightly striped knee-high socks or tons of different colored bracelets or a dress that looked like it might have been a nightgown. Once she'd even come to school wearing a sparkly rhinestone tiara. But it wasn't just her clothes that were strange. She always seemed to be off in her own world, either reading sci-fi books in a corner somewhere or else doodling in a sketch pad. While Jenna was one of the most popular girls in the school, Amanda was one of the least.

"I like her," Naeemah said. "And I like the way she is outfitted. She does not look like the rest of your classmates."

"You can say that again," Keisha replied.

"She does not look like the rest of your classmates," Naeemah repeated obediently.

"No, Naeemah. I—" Keisha shook her head. "I really need to teach you more expressions."

"Perhaps you can give me a lesson after lunch," Naeemah suggested. "At this moment, let us go sit with Amanda."

Keisha took one more look around and sighed. "Fine," she said. Amanda really was her only option. As they approached the table, Keisha took note of her current outfit.

She was wearing black lace-up boots, black jeans, and a black long-sleeved stretch shirt. At her waist, she had cinched a piece of fabric with a safety pin. It was bright orange with some kind of bleached-out pattern running through it, and the way she was wearing it, it looked like a cross between a miniskirt and a too-small bath towel. Her hair, which was long and wavy when she wore it down, had been wound into two tight buns that resembled horns, and she was wearing a short necklace with some kind of Japanese symbol dangling off of it.

"Hi," Keisha said as she set her tray down. "What's up?" Out of the corner of her eye she caught Naeemah gazing confusedly up at the ceiling.

"Not much," Amanda said. "I was just thinking—oh, hey, Sam," she said as a boy with shaggy blond hair joined them. He was a seventh grader who, along with Amanda, was considered a bit of an oddity at Adams Middle School. "Do you know Keisha Johnson?" Amanda asked.

Sam sort of shrugged. "I think I've seen you around," he said. "I'm Sam."

"Hi," Keisha said. She didn't bother to explain to him that she, along with everyone else, already knew who he was because he was so strange. He dressed mostly in black or other dark colors, but it was his hair that most people noticed, mainly because it was so big.

Typically when people grew their hair long, it grew *down*, but Sam's just seemed to keep growing *out*. It wasn't curly or anything, like Keisha's, it was just . . . huge. And Sam never seemed to make any sort of attempt to contain it. Some of the boys, like Noah, referred to him as Einstein because of it. Keisha had always thought it was kind of funny, but she felt a little guilty for laughing about it now that she was sitting across from him.

"So how come you're not sitting with the varsity squad today?" Sam asked, nodding toward the table where Jenna, Emily, and Sarah had been joined by Noah, his buddies, and even a few seventh and eighth graders.

Keisha gazed over at her friends to see them laughing hysterically while two of the guys threw mock punches at each other. Obviously they weren't itching anymore. Or missing her— if they'd even noticed that she was gone.

"You don't want to sit with them anyway," Amanda assured her. "They're gingerbread people."

"Gingerbread people?" Keisha echoed. She glanced down at Naeemah. This time they were equally lost.

"All the same," Amanda explained. "Like they were made with cookie cutters."

Keisha chuckled. She'd never heard the expression before, but she liked it.

"So, anyway," Amanda went on, "I was thinking about your detention."

Keisha snorted. "Yeah, I've been thinking about it, too."

"You got a detention?" Sam asked.

"Yeah, from Mrs. MacKnight," Keisha said.

"You mean Mrs. Mac*Nightmare*," Sam said.

"Hey, that's good," Keisha replied, chuckling.

"Sam's great with nicknames," Amanda said. "But anyway, about your detention. I think you should fight it."

"She has fire in her eyes," Naeemah said. "Like the great goddess Hathor who raised the sun up to Heaven."

Keisha raised one eyebrow at Naeemah, and then turned back to Amanda. To her surprise, however, Amanda was now staring at her shoulder—or rather at the place on her shoulder where Naeemah was standing—with a bewildered expression. Keisha glanced back at Naeemah, but she was gone. *What the—?* she wondered.

"Keisha?" Amanda said. "What's wrong?"

"Huh? Oh, nothing," Keisha said. She shook her head to regain her train of thought. She'd have to find out where Naeemah was later.

"So you think I should *what*?" she asked.

"Fight the detention," Amanda said. "It wasn't your fault that MacKnight tripped, and she can't prove that you did it on purpose."

"I didn't trip her," Keisha said. "She just fell."

"Exactly," Amanda replied. "And she can't give you a detention for that."

"But she did," Keisha said.

"Which is why you should fight it," Amanda insisted.

Keisha ate a spoonful of her yogurt and thought it over. "I don't know," she said.

"You tripped MacNightmare?" Sam said, setting down his fork.

"*No*," Keisha replied. "She just fell. Right next to me."

"I wish I'd been there to see that," Sam said, laughing. "That must have been great. Did she catch herself or did she totally wipe out?"

"Sam," Amanda said. "That's not nice. She could have been hurt."

"You're the one who's calling her a klutz," Sam protested.

"No, I'm not. I'm just saying that Keisha should fight the detention because—"

"Because MacNightmare's a klutz."

"No, because—"

"Hey, guys," Keisha interrupted. "You don't have to argue about it. I'm not going to fight the detention anyway."

"Are you sure?" Amanda asked. "I think you could win."

Sam laughed. "Amanda's all about fighting the power."

Amanda scowled at him. "I just don't think it was fair, that's all," she said.

"Neither do I," Keisha replied, "but it's easier to just go this afternoon and get it over with. Besides, I'd probably have to stay after school if I wanted to fight it, too."

"I guess," Amanda said.

"I just wish my mom didn't have to close her shop to come pick me up afterward. She's not going to be happy with me," Keisha said.

"What about your dad?" Sam asked.

"He drives a truck. It's hard to get in touch with him during the day," Keisha said.

"Hey! Sam and I are staying after school to work on a project in the art room, and my mom's picking us up at four. We could give you a ride home."

"Are you sure?" Keisha asked. Then she glanced over at her friends again. They were still laughing and having a good time. She couldn't help wondering what they would say if they saw her hanging out with Amanda and Sam. Whatever it was, it probably wouldn't be nice.

"Yeah, no problem," Amanda said. "Your mom runs that store, Something Old, Something New, right?"

"Right," Keisha replied, surprised.

"I love that place. Sam and I stopped in there a couple of weekends ago and I've been dying to go back."

"Yeah, there's some really cool stuff in there," Sam agreed.

"Thanks," Keisha said.

"We go right by there on our way home," Amanda said. "It would be easy for my mom to drop you off."

"Are you sure?" Keisha asked.

"Yep," Amanda said. "So just come down to the art room when your detention's over, okay?"

"Okay," Keisha said. Keisha was sure that her mother would be less angry about the detention if she didn't have to leave work to pick her up.

Amanda and Sam picked up their trays just as the bell was ringing at the end of lunch. "See you later, Keisha," Amanda called.

"Yeah, see you later," Keisha replied. Then

she reached into the front pocket of her Boston College sweatshirt. She'd felt something squirming around in there for the last ten minutes and she was pretty sure she knew what it was.

Carefully, she extracted Naeemah and set her on the table. "Why did you disappear all of a sudden?"

Naeemah brought her hands together in front of her chest and bowed. "I am sorry to have abandoned you, Keisha, but it was that girl."

"Amanda? What about her?" Keisha asked.

"She saw me. I am sure of it."

CHAPTER
Six

"Are you sure she will not tell others about me?" Naeemah asked for the eighteenth time that afternoon. "I do not wish to be taken away and studied for science."

She and Keisha had stopped in the rest-room on their way to Mrs. MacKnight's room for detention, and Naeemah had been fretting nonstop about the possibility of having been seen by Amanda.

"Don't worry. Nobody's going to study you for science," she assured the tiny girl as she scrubbed her hands under the warm water. "Especially since I don't even think Amanda saw you. She would have screamed or jumped or said something if she had. She just happened to be looking in your direction, that's all."

Keisha pumped the paper-towel dispenser

twice and dried her hands on the rough brown paper. "I don't think you have anything to worry about."

"Very well," Naeemah said. "I shall put my mind at ease."

"No," Keisha said, shaking her head. "Not 'Very well, I shall put my mind at ease.' You should say, 'Cool. I won't sweat it.'"

"What does this mean?"

"It's slang for *I shall put my mind at ease*," Keisha said. "You know, like the other ones I wrote down for you in my notebook during language arts—*what's up*, *chill out*, remember those?"

"Ah, yes," Naeemah said, brightening. After Keisha had explained a few words and phrases to her, she had been excited to learn more. "All right. I shall use the slang." Naeemah stood up straight, beaming as she spoke. "Cool," she said. "I won't sweat."

"I won't sweat *it*," Keisha corrected.

"I won't sweat *it*," Naeemah echoed.

"Good enough," Keisha said. "Now let's go get this detention thing over with."

Naeemah hopped onto Keisha's shoulder and the two of them headed for Mrs. MacKnight's room. "Here goes nothing," Keisha said, opening the door.

"Good afternoon, Miss Johnson," Mrs. MacKnight said, glancing at the clock. "Your detention will officially begin at two-thirty and last for one hour. You may sit down now if you like, but you should know that I will not be dismissing you prior to three-thirty simply because you've shown up five minutes early."

Keisha considered walking back into the hall to enjoy her last five minutes of freedom, but she figured that killing time outside the door would be pretty much the same as killing time inside the room. "Okay," she said, walking to her usual homeroom seat.

For the next four and a half minutes, she and Naeemah waited silently. While Mrs. MacKnight corrected papers, Keisha thought of some more slang terms and expressions to write down for Naeemah and added them to her notebook while Naeemah read along. They managed to cover *hip*, *hip-hop*, *hot*, *posse*, and *peeps* in that time. While Keisha had to remain silent, Naeemah, who knew Mrs. MacKnight couldn't hear her, was anxious to try her new words.

"Your friends believe that Noah Carpenter is hot, do they not?" she asked. "But I am not fond of Emily, Sarah, and Jenna. I think you should find some new peeps." Naeemah smiled smugly, proud of her word usage. "Perhaps Amanda and Sam could be part of your new possum?" she suggested.

Keisha almost lost it, but she managed to cough a few times to cover her laughter. When she had regained her composure, she added *lose it* to her list of definitions.

"All right, Miss Johnson," Mrs. MacKnight said. "Your detention has now officially begun. Please come to the front row and occupy the seat nearest my desk. I'll give you work to keep you busy for the next hour."

"That's okay, Mrs. MacKnight," Keisha said. "I brought my homework."

Mrs. MacKnight fixed Keisha with a stern stare, her beady black eyes boring holes into Keisha's head. "I do not allow students to do homework in detention," she said. "This is not your time to use as you wish. This is time that you owe to me, and you will use it to help me complete my work."

"Oh," Keisha said. She walked to the front of the room and sat down heavily.

"First," Mrs. MacKnight said, "you will go through these blank calendar pages and fill out the information for the rest of the school year: months, days, dates, holidays, et cetera. Then, when you have finished that, you will sort through this pile of articles, separating them by subject so that I may file them. Of course, if you finish that before the time is up, you can do the filing, and if you should finish that as well, don't worry—I have plenty more for you to do."

Mrs. MacKnight set the calendar pages and the stack of articles on the desk next to Keisha and then handed her four colored pens. "I would like the names of the months written in blue, the days of the week in green, the numbered dates in black, and all holidays marked in red."

For a moment, Keisha just stared. Wasn't there some kind of child-labor law to prevent teachers from using students as their personal slaves?

"What are you waiting for, Miss Johnson? Get to work," Mrs. MacKnight said. She stood over Keisha with her arms crossed, waiting, until Keisha finally reached out and grabbed the first calendar page. Under Mrs. MacKnight's watchful eyes, she began to write *September* across the top of the page in the designated space, then switched to green and began marking the days of the week.

"The week begins with Sunday, not Monday, Miss Johnson. Please start again."

Keisha swallowed hard. This detention business was way more intense than she had expected. Mrs. MacKnight watched as Keisha began a new page, making sure that she started the week with Sunday, and then returned to her desk to correct more papers.

"Great Horus!" Naeemah exclaimed, watching her walk away. "This woman is wicked. She needs to . . . to . . ." she paused and pointed at Mrs. MacKnight before issuing her command. "Chill out," Naeemah pronounced.

Keisha met Naeemah's eyes and signaled her agreement with a slight raise of her eyebrows. If her little friend could use her magic to get Mrs. MacKnight to lighten up, she was all for it. But when she glanced at Mrs. MacKnight, she saw that Naeemah was still far from having her magic under control.

"It's getting a bit nippy in here, isn't it?" Mrs. MacKnight commented. She pulled a cardigan from her large canvas bag and wrapped it around her shoulders.

"Oh, my," Naeemah said. "That's not what I meant. I did not intend to make her cold."

Keisha just smirked.

"But I suppose her body temperature will return to normal," Naeemah went on, "considering the fact that my magic does not seem to last very long."

Keisha gave Naeemah a slight nod.

"It is most unfortunate that I do not possess more power," Naeemah said. "That woman really does need to relax." She pointed at Mrs. MacKnight again. "If I could, I would make her pleasant, kind, and cheerful twenty-one seven."

Again, Keisha had to hide a budding laugh. She tapped her notebook, pointing to the phrase *twenty-four seven*, so that Naeemah could see that she had left out three hours per day, but before Naeemah had a chance to look, Mrs. MacKnight was standing over Keisha once again.

Keisha looked up slowly. *What now?* she wondered. She was still on January, but she hadn't messed up at all as far as she could tell.

"That is really beautiful, Keisha," Mrs. MacKnight said, smiling down at the calendar page, "and I really appreciate you taking the time to help me out, but I don't want to keep you any later. I'm sure you have plenty of homework to do, and you probably want to get home and have a nice afternoon snack or something, don't you?"

Keisha's mouth dropped open.

"She has lost her brain," Naeemah said.

"Keisha? Are you all right, dear?"

The sound of Mrs. MacKnight referring to her as *dear* snapped Keisha out of her stupor. "Um, yeah. I'm fine, Mrs. MacKnight."

"Are you sure? You look a little faint. Why don't I get you a cookie. I always keep a secret stash in my desk. Hold on just one minute."

Keisha watched, dumbfounded, as Mrs. MacKnight hurried over to her desk and removed a box of cookies from the bottom drawer. "They're chocolate mint. Is that all right?" Mrs. MacKnight asked.

"Yeah. Sure," Keisha replied. Her newly transformed teacher placed two on her desk.

"Thanks," Keisha said.

"You're welcome, Keisha," Mrs. MacKnight said. "And thank you for helping me get my calendar started. It was so kind of you to come in this afternoon."

"Um, no problem," Keisha said.

Mrs. MacKnight collected all of the calendar pages, the articles, and the pens from Keisha and brought them back to her desk. Then she looked at Keisha expectantly. "You can go," she repeated. "Unless, of course, there's something you wanted to talk to me about."

"No, thanks," Keisha said, shaking her head.

"I'm . . . all set." She gathered up her things and made her way to the door, glancing back at Mrs. MacKnight every few steps. She was afraid that at any moment she might change back into her old self and accuse Keisha of trying to sneak out of detention early. But as Keisha exited the room and closed the door, Mrs. MacKnight simply smiled at her and waved.

"Whoa!" Keisha said when she and Naeemah were safely down the hall and around the corner. "That was weird!"

"Indeed it was," Naeemah agreed. "Do you think the magic will last this time?"

"I don't know," Keisha said, "but the expression is twenty-*four* seven, not twenty-one seven. So even if it does, there are still going to be three hours every day when she's not pleasant and kind and whatever else you said."

"Cheerful," Naeemah put in.

"Whatever," Keisha said. "I just hope I'm not around during her downtime."

In the art room, Keisha found Amanda and Sam at work on a large papier-mâché palm tree. "Wow," Keisha said as she walked in. "That's cool. What's it for?"

Sam, who was affixing a papier-mâché

coconut to one of the papier-mâché fronds, looked over at her. "It's for that dance the PTO is sponsoring next week."

"What dance?" Keisha asked.

"The multicultural one," Amanda replied, but Keisha was still drawing a blank. Amanda shook her head. "I *told* my mother she needed to put up more posters. No one knows about it."

"Amanda's mom is in charge of publicity," Sam said as he wired his coconut in place.

"And Sam's mom is handling the refreshments," Amanda said, touching up the brown paint on the trunk.

"They're both part of the PTO," Sam said. "You know—the Parent-Teacher Organization. Amanda's mom is president, and my dad's in charge of fund-raising. So they enlisted us to help out with decorations."

"You're making all of the decorations?" Keisha asked. She checked to see if Naeemah was as impressed as she was, but Naeemah had disappeared again—no doubt because she was afraid that Amanda was going to sell her to a scientist somewhere.

"We're helping Ms. Rainey," Amanda said. "She's having the eighth graders do a lot of the decorations in art class, but Sam and I are working with her on the bigger projects, like this palm tree."

"Do you want to help?" Sam asked.

"Me?"

"Sure," Amanda said, glancing at the clock. "We've got another hour before my mom will be here to pick us up."

"Might as well make yourself useful," Sam suggested, handing Keisha a paintbrush.

From inside her pocket, Keisha heard a muffled, "I knew school would be fun!" and grinned.

Amanda squinted over at her and cocked her head. "What did you say?" she asked.

Keisha's eyebrows shot up. "Nothing. Why?"

Amanda looked around the room as though she were searching for a specific object, then gazed back at Keisha. "I just thought I heard something," she said.

Keisha watched as Amanda went back to painting. Had she actually heard Naeemah's voice? And if so, how? Why would Amanda be able to hear and see the tiny Egyptian when no one else could?

"Well, what are you waiting for?" Sam asked, glancing toward Keisha.

Keisha shrugged. "What should I do?" she asked.

"I'm sorry, I should have explained," Sam said. "What you do is take that funny thing I gave you," he went on, pointing to the paintbrush, "and dip it in the bucket here. Then, when it's good and covered, dab at the branches with it and it will make them green. It's complicated, I know, but I think you can handle it."

Keisha tilted her head and half-scowled, half-smiled at him.

"Got it?" he asked with a grin.

"Yes." Keisha walked over to the tree and started working.

Sam glanced at Amanda. "And you said she was too cool," he said.

"I did not!" Amanda cried. "You're such a troublemaker, Sam." She shook her paintbrush at him, covering his face in tiny green flecks.

"Hey!"

"You deserved that," Amanda said. "Don't pay attention to him, Keisha. He's always trying to get people going."

"Right now, the only thing I want to get going is the two of you," Sam said. "We still have another palm tree, an elephant, and a three-toed sloth to paint."

Keisha dipped her brush in the green paint, working on the branch next to Amanda's. As she painted, she looked around the room and saw the other papier-mâché sculptures Sam had mentioned, along with some that had already been painted. There was a statue of a veiled woman with finger cymbals as well as a building with a large domed roof and four smaller domes in a square around it.

"Are those for the dance, too?" Keisha asked.

"Mm-hm."

She looked at them again, wondering how they fit in with the palm trees, the elephant, and the sloth. "What are they?"

"That one's some kind of temple in Sudan," Sam said, pointing to the building. "I can't remember what it's called. Ms. Rainey did it. And the woman is a belly dancer. What country is she supposed to be from, Amanda?"

Amanda squinted one eye while she thought. "Lebanon, I think," she said.

"These sure are strange decorations," Keisha observed. "What kind of dance did you say this was?"

"A multicultural one," Amanda replied.

"What does that mean?"

"It means it's supposed to include a bunch of different cultures," Sam said.

"But why elephants and palm trees and everything?" Keisha asked.

"To represent the different countries all the kids in our district come from," Amanda explained. "The dance is being held at Adams, but it's for all the middle schools in the area. Lincoln, Washington—"

"Monroe," Sam added.

"Yeah, and there are two or three others, too," Amanda said.

"So the palm trees are for . . . ?"

"The Caribbean," Amanda said. "There are students from Haiti, the Dominican Republic, Jamaica, and Puerto Rico."

"And the elephant?"

"Sudan," Sam answered.

"What about the sloth?" Keisha asked.

"Brazil," Amanda said. "And I think we have some parrots from the rain forest, too."

"Yup," Sam said. "They're in the back." He finished wiring on his last coconut and walked over to the other unpainted sculptures. "I'm going to start painting the sloth, okay?"

"Sure," Amanda said with a nod. "I'll start on the elephant. Are you okay to finish this tree?" she asked Keisha.

"Sure. And then I can start on the other one if

you want," Keisha offered. This multicultural dance sounded like a cool idea. She was psyched that she was getting a chance to help out with it.

Keisha fingered the silver bracelet around her wrist, the one that Jasmine had sent to her. Maybe it really *was* lucky. After all, she'd met Sam and Amanda the day after she'd received it in the mail, and now she was working on a really cool project with them. And, of course, Naeemah had popped out of the fairy tale book just a few hours after Keisha had first put the bracelet on.

Naeemah, Keisha thought, glancing down at the lump in her sweatshirt pocket. Without her, Keisha may never have been given the detention that got Amanda so fired up, and she probably wouldn't have sat with Amanda and Sam at lunch, either. Or gotten out of Mrs. MacKnight's room early enough to work with them.

She glanced down at her bracelet again, touching each of the four charms in turn. Could such a simple piece of jewelry have had anything to do with Naeemah showing up when she did? Keisha wondered. Jasmine had said it would bring her good luck, but she hadn't mentioned anything about a two-inch-tall Egyptian teenager. *Still*, Keisha thought, *it might be worth asking.*

CHAPTER
Seven

To: jazzypdesigns@nh.teletron.com
From: keishaj123@ma.inet.com
Subject: re: thanks!

Hey, Jasmine,
About that bracelet—when you said "good luck," what did you mean? I've made some new friends, and one of them is really . . . unique. And short. Maybe I can tell you more about her in another e-mail. But first, can you tell me what kind of good luck it brought you?

TTFN,
Keisha

"Is there anyone who has not handed in a card?" Mrs. MacKnight asked the next day in homeroom. Reluctantly, Jesse Hunter raised his hand. "Mr. Hunter," Mrs. MacKnight said, shaking her head. "I guess you'll just have to . . . have one of my homemade chocolate chip cookies!" She produced a plate from behind her desk and beamed at Jesse.

The entire room went silent.

"Don't worry," Mrs. MacKnight said. "There are enough for everybody. And, Jesse, you can just bring me that card tomorrow, okay?"

"O-okay," Jesse replied. He looked around the room suspiciously, as if searching for hidden cameras.

"I can't believe it," Keisha whispered to Naeemah. "The magic is still working. I wonder how long it will last."

"I believe I did say *permanently,* when I made the declaration," Naeemah whispered from inside Keisha's backpack. Amanda sat three rows away in homeroom, but Naeemah didn't want to take any chances.

Of course, she didn't want to go so far as to stay home from school. She had enjoyed her first day too much for that. But Naeemah had decided to stay out of sight for the most part and to talk as little as possible—especially when Amanda was around.

Keisha had to agree that keeping a low profile was probably a pretty good idea. After all, if Amanda had seen or heard her, it was possible that others might, too, and Keisha figured the fewer people who knew about Naeemah, the better.

While Mrs. MacKnight made her way around with the cookies, everyone in the class was whispering about her strange behavior.

"What's up with that?" Jesse Hunter mouthed after he'd received his cookie.

"These are actually good," Patrick Coyne muttered.

Keisha received her cookie and broke off a crumb for Naeemah. They bit into their respective pieces and exchanged a surprised look. "This is freezing!" Naeemah exclaimed.

Keisha squinted down at her. "*What?*" she whispered.

"I thought that if cool was good, freezing would be even better. Is that not how it works?" Naeemah asked.

"Not quite," Keisha replied with a smile. "But good try."

"Excuse me, Mrs. MacKnight?"

Keisha turned toward the door to see the only person who could ruin this moment for her: Jenna Scott. And to make matters worse, Emily and Sarah were hovering just outside the door, waiting for her.

"Jenna," Mrs. MacKnight chimed. "Would you like a cookie, dear?"

Jenna glanced toward the door to see if her friends had heard Mrs. MacKnight's offer. Sure enough, Emily and Sarah were right there, peeking around the side of the door with wide eyes. Keisha watched them closely, waiting for them to look at her and smile or wave.

But they never glanced in her direction. They were too focused on their heroic Jenna and the strangely behaving Mrs. MacKnight.

"It's a family recipe," Mrs. MacKnight said, passing the cookie plate under Jenna's nose.

Jenna winced, then raised her brows and gazed around the room. She looked over-alert and nervous like an outcast who'd just stumbled into a circle of popular kids. It was so strange to see the ever-confident Jenna Scott looking so uncomfortable. Keisha almost felt sorry for her. Almost.

"Um, no, thanks," Jenna said. "I just came in to—"

"Are you sure?" Mrs. MacKnight held out the plate to Jenna. "They're homemade."

"They're really good," Jesse Hunter added.

Jenna pressed her lips together. "Thanks," she said warily, "but I just brushed my teeth."

"Oh, Jenna," Mrs. MacKnight said with a motherly grin. She wrapped her free arm around Jenna's shoulders and gave her a squeeze. Jenna's eyes nearly popped out of her head, and Emily and Sarah out in the hall looked like they'd just seen an army of ghosts. Everyone in the classroom began tittering. They'd never seen Mrs. MacKnight give *anyone* a hug, and the fact that it was Jenna Scott, who was cooler than cool, made it all the more hilarious. Keisha covered her mouth to keep from laughing out loud.

"You just brushed your teeth," Mrs. MacKnight chuckled. "That's so sweet. Here—why don't I wrap one up in a napkin and you can save it for later." She gave Jenna a final squeeze, then went to her desk to package the cookie. Jenna remained where she was, stunned into silence.

"Here you go," Mrs. MacKnight said, handing her a neatly wrapped bundle. "I put a few in there for you to share with your friends," she added, nodding toward the hall. Jenna accepted the package, but didn't move. "Now, what was it you came in here for?" Mrs. MacKnight asked.

"Huh? Oh," Jenna stammered. She'd totally

lost her usual composure. "I'm collecting the attendance slips today."

"Oh, my," exclaimed Mrs. MacKnight. "I was so excited about the cookies that I completely forgot about attendance. If you'll just wait a moment—"

"I can come back," Jenna said, and before Mrs. MacKnight could argue, she was out the door and down the hall, with Emily and Sarah close at her heels.

"Looks like your upgrade to Mrs. MacNightmare was too much for the gingerbread people," Keisha whispered as she leaned over her backpack.

"Upgrade?" Naeemah asked. "Oh, you are referring to her improved disposition? Yes, I believe Jenna was rather freaked up."

"*Out*," Keisha muttered. "Freaked *out*."

"Yes," Naeemah agreed. "That, too."

"And then Jenna sprinted out of the room," Amanda said. "MacKnight had to have Jesse Hunter take the attendance slip to the office for her." Keisha took a bite of her apple, enjoying the replay Amanda was giving Sam during lunch. It was great to remember the frightened, *freaked-up* look on Jenna's face.

Sam laughed. "That's great," he said. "I wish I'd been there for that, too. MacNightmare sure is making things interesting this year." He stuffed a few fries in his mouth and swallowed them in one gulp. "So what's up with her, anyway? I was in her homeroom last year and she never made us cookies."

"I don't know," Amanda said. "It's like all of a sudden she's a totally different person."

Keisha glanced down at Naeemah, who was hiding out in her lap where Amanda wouldn't be able to see her—if, in fact, she even could.

"Weird," Sam said.

"Weirder," Keisha replied, pointing just over his shoulder. Jenna Scott was headed straight for them. As she approached, she looked to her left and right, finally coming to a halt at the end of the table. "I have a bunch of posters for you in my locker," she mumbled, half of her attention focused on Amanda, the other half on the people passing by in back of her. "When can you come get them?"

"Hi, Jenna," Amanda said. "It's nice to see you, too."

Jenna rolled her eyes. "Can you stop by my locker after school?"

"Sure," Amanda said. "And I'll try not to let

anyone see me, okay?"

"Whatever," Jenna replied, heaving a sigh. Then she turned and walked away.

Keisha screwed up her face. "What was *that* about?" she asked.

"Jenna's mom is in the PTO with my mom, and her uncle has a print shop, so he printed all the posters for the dance for free. Mrs. Scott must have made Jenna bring them to school today so I could give them to my mom."

"She was rather rude, though," Naeemah said from Keisha's lap.

Amanda shrugged, but then Sam stuffed a handful of fries into his mouth and nodded in agreement.

Keisha and Naeemah exchanged shocked glances. Amanda had definitely heard Naeemah! And it appeared that Sam had heard her, too!

"She used to be really nice," Amanda went on. Obviously, she had mistaken Naeemah's voice for Keisha's, and Sam was too focused on finishing his fries to have noticed anything. *Phew,* Keisha thought, giving Naeemah a warning glance. Naeemah placed her hand over her mouth to indicate that she planned to remain silent.

"We live practically next door to each other,

and when we were little, Jenna, Sam, and I used to play together all the time."

"That was when we were at Franklin, and Jenna was going to Cathedral," Sam said. Franklin was one of the elementary schools in the North End, and Cathedral was a private school in Brookline. Keisha had attended Pierce Elementary along with Sarah and Emily, so they hadn't met Sam, Amanda, or Jenna until fifth grade, when the students from all the smaller neighborhood elementary schools merged into Adams Middle School.

"Yeah," Amanda agreed. "Jenna went to a private elementary school, and Sam's a year older, so we didn't see one another much during the day. But we always hung out in the afternoons and on weekends and stuff—until Jenna and I started at Adams in fifth grade."

"She ditched us in a matter of seconds," Sam said.

"Mm-hm," Amanda agreed. "It was like suddenly one day she realized she could be really popular."

"And she decided that being friends with us would just hold her back," Sam put in.

Amanda glanced down at her outfit—a thick cuff bracelet on each wrist, pink-and-green polyester thrift-store blouse, along with faded navy corduroys and black boots. Then she glanced at Sam's black Montreal Jazz Festival T-shirt, blue jeans, work boots, and of course, his gravity-defying halo of hair. "We're not exactly J. Crew material," she joked, "but we still live in Jenna's neighborhood and our parents are friends, so sometimes Jenna has to talk to us."

"And she hates it," Sam said emphatically.

"That's awful," Keisha said. On her lap, Naeemah nodded, her hand still clapped over her mouth. "So is Jenna helping out with the dance at all?"

"No way," Amanda said. "Jenna thinks the whole multicultural dance thing is lame. At least, that's what she told me one day when her mom sent her over to drop off some stuff for my mother. I asked her if she was planning to go to it and she said that any dance that was planned by parents and teachers was bound to be boring."

"Wow," Keisha said. She looked over to where Jenna was sitting with Emily and Sarah and the same group of boys who had sat with them yesterday. "I can't believe you guys used to be friends with her."

"Best friends," Amanda said.

"But you seem so . . . different," Keisha replied. At least, she, Emily, and Sarah had always had a lot in common.

Amanda shrugged. "We weren't," she said. "But people change."

"Some more than others," Sam added.

Keisha poked at a kernel of corn with her fork. Was that what was happening with her, Emily, and Sarah? Were they changing? Or was it her? It made her sad to think that they might never be friends again. Surely that couldn't be true.

She glanced over at her friends. They were sitting on either side of Luke Davidson and giggling shamelessly. They hadn't spoken to her since yesterday's lunch fiasco, and neither of them had been on the bus that morning—they had gotten a ride with Jenna. Keisha knew because she'd seen Jenna's mom drop the three of them off at the semicircle by the main entrance to the school.

So that was that. Emily and Sarah were Jenna Scott's new best friends, and if they were missing Keisha at all, they certainly weren't showing it.

"Hey, I'll catch you guys after school," Sam said, getting up to leave. "I have to hit the library so I can finish up my book report before class."

"I'll go with you, Sam," Amanda said. "I want to see if Mrs. Barber has any new library books. You want to come, Keisha?"

Keisha shook her head. "No, thanks."

"Are you all right?" Amanda asked.

"Yeah," Keisha said. "I just . . . want to finish my food."

Amanda glanced down at the mystery meat that made up that day's meal. "Good luck with that," she said, grimacing.

When they were gone, Keisha poked at one of her green beans, replaying in her mind what Amanda had said about Jenna. Was it possible that Emily and Sarah would one day hate the idea of being seen talking to Keisha? Did they already? Keisha wasn't sure, but that definitely seemed to be the way things were headed.

"Phew. The coast is clean," Naeemah said.

"Clear," Keisha corrected her.

"Ah, yes, the coast is *clear*," Naeemah said, climbing up Keisha's arm and leaping onto the table. "Either way, I believe we have established the fact that Amanda can indeed hear me."

Keisha nodded. "I think Sam can, too," she said. Then she poked at another green bean.

"The boy hears me as well?" Naeemah cried. When Keisha didn't respond, Naeemah took a few steps closer and gazed up at her face. "Why are you not concerned?" she asked. "What is up?"

Keisha put down her fork and pushed her tray out of the way. She nodded toward Jenna, Emily, and Sarah, who were all laughing together as if they'd just heard the funniest joke in the entire world.

"That's what's up," she said. "I've lost my friends."

Naeemah folded her arms. "In my opinion, they were not very good friends. Sam and Amanda are much kinder."

"But they weren't always like this, Naeemah," Keisha said. "We used to have a lot of fun—we grew up together." Keisha removed her napkin from her lap and crumpled it into a ball on her tray. "But now it's like they've forgotten all about me."

"I'm sure they have not forgotten you," Naeemah said.

Keisha snorted. "Well, they definitely don't seem to be missing me," she said.

"Perhaps that is because they do not realize they should be," Naeemah suggested.

"What do you mean?"

"You are aware of the distance between you because you are the one drifting away," Naeemah said. "But it is possible they have not yet realized you are gone. If they did, perhaps they would come after you."

Keisha looked down at her little friend, noticing the melancholy look in her eyes. She looked, once again, like that girl in the picture sailing down the river all alone. "Are you sure you're talking about *me*?" Keisha asked.

"I am talking about both of us. I ran away from my village, and you are running away from your friends."

"I'm not running away," Keisha protested. "I'm being pushed away."

"Perhaps it is a little of both," Naeemah suggested. "In any case, I believe you should talk with your friends and tell them how you are feeling."

Keisha winced. "I can't—"

"You must try," Naeemah said. "I ran away from my problems, and now I can never go back."

"Yeah, but—"

"Running away has not solved my problems," Naeemah went on. "I miss my family terribly, and I am no closer to becoming a doctor here than I was there. In fact, I am probably even farther from my goal." She glanced up at Keisha with a half smirk. "I do not believe I could conduct a proper medical examination on people of your size."

Keisha chuckled. "No, probably not," she agreed.

"If I could choose the end of my story," Naeemah went on, growing serious again, "I would go back to my village and tell my parents how I feel. They would not make me marry against my will. I know they would not."

"But how would you become a doctor?"

"I am not sure," Naeemah admitted. "But I know now that running away is not the answer, which is why you must make one more effort with your friends before you give up on them. Perhaps if you are honest with them, they will surprise you."

Keisha watched Emily and Sarah as they picked up their lunch things and got ready to go. Maybe Naeemah was right. Maybe talking with Sarah and Emily would make a difference. Maybe, just maybe, if she could get Sarah and Emily alone for a minute, she could let them know how she was feeling and convince them that their friendship was worth salvaging.

"All right," Keisha said, glancing down at her littlest friend. "I'll give it a try."

Naeemah clapped her hands together. "Wonderful," she said, but Keisha wasn't sure how wonderful it was going to be. She watched Emily and Sarah as they bounced out of the cafeteria behind Jenna and her band of boys. They didn't exactly seem to be aching for Keisha's presence.

CHAPTER
Eight

"This is stupid," Keisha said. She turned around and started to leave.

"You must speak with them," Naeemah urged. "If you do not, you will always wonder what might have been."

Stopping in her tracks, Keisha turned back toward Ms. Garcia's door. For some reason, Ms. Garcia was keeping her homeroom late today. Keisha couldn't see much through the narrow window in the door from where she was standing, but she was sure they were doing something fun—they always were.

Of course, lately, things had been pretty entertaining in Mrs. MacKnight's class. Cookies during homeroom, games to learn about ancient Greece in social studies, and Adams Middle School trivia for candy and movie passes during afternoon homeroom. Keisha really couldn't complain, except for the fact that she was still separated from her two best friends, who seemed to be growing more distant with each passing day.

The knob on Ms. Garcia's door started to turn, and Keisha's heart fluttered. "I can't do this," she murmured, and once again she turned to walk away.

"Yes, you can," Naeemah insisted. She was riding in the pocket of Keisha's short-sleeved button-front shirt. "It is the right thing to do," she continued. "You must confront your peeps."

Keisha felt a tiny grin forming in spite of her anxiety. But as the door to Ms. Garcia's room opened, the smile vanished from her face. Emily and Sarah were headed toward the door, but Jenna was right beside them.

"This will not do," Naeemah said. She stood up tall and leaned out of Keisha's pocket, pointing at Jenna. "I wish *she* would go back into the room," she said.

"Jenna?" Ms. Garcia called. "Could you come here for a minute?"

"I'll catch up to you," Jenna said to Sarah and Emily.

Keisha looked down at Naeemah and

mouthed, "Thanks." Then, gathering up her courage, she approached her friends.

"Hey, Emily. Hey, Sarah," she said, trying to keep the tremor out of her voice. Her friends turned toward her, and stopped. Both of them looked back over their shoulders into Ms. Garcia's room. *Probably to see where Jenna is,* Keisha thought. It was pathetic—like they couldn't make a move without her. *Or like they're already ashamed to be seen with me.*

"Keisha," Emily said, her tone less than excited. "What's up?"

"Not much," Keisha said. "I was just wondering if—"

"We can't hang out this afternoon," Emily interrupted. "We're going to the mall with Jenna."

"We'd ask you to come," Sarah said, "but it was Jenna's idea to go, so—" Sarah held up both her palms and shrugged.

"I know, you can't just invite people along," Keisha said.

"Right," Sarah agreed. She looked at Keisha awkwardly for a moment, then both she and Emily glanced over their shoulders toward Ms. Garcia's room.

Unbelievable, Keisha thought. They couldn't even face her. This was ridiculous. She was about to tell them to just forget it, when she glanced down and saw Naeemah's hopeful face. Keisha closed her eyes and sighed. She had to do it. She had to give it her best effort. If she didn't, she'd always be wondering if there was something she could have said or done differently.

She took a deep breath and addressed her friends. "It's not about this afternoon," she said. "I'm busy, anyway."

"Oh," Emily and Sarah said at the same time, turning back toward Keisha. Both of them looked immensely relieved.

"So, then, . . . what's going on?" Sarah asked.

Keisha shifted her weight. "Well," she started, trying to find the right words, "it's just that, I wanted to talk to you . . . about how things have been getting kind of weird lately."

Emily and Sarah glanced at each other, then back at Keisha, their eyes narrowed. "What do you mean?" Sarah asked.

"Well, it's just that—" Getting the words out was even harder than Keisha had thought it was going to be. "I kind of feel like, I don't know, like we don't hang out that much anymore."

"Really?" Sarah asked.

"We spent last Saturday at your mom's store," Emily said.

"I know," Keisha said, "but—" She wasn't sure how to express what she was feeling.

"But what?" Emily asked.

"I don't know," Keisha hesitated. "I guess it just kind of seems like things have changed somehow. It's like" —here came the tough part— "now that you're hanging out with Jenna so much, I sort of feel like you guys don't want me around anymore."

Emily took a deep breath and looked down the hall toward her locker. "That's not true," she said without meeting Keisha's eyes. Keisha turned to Sarah, but Sarah just kept focusing on her feet, which she was shifting from side to side. *That's not true? That's all Emily could say?* It wasn't exactly convincing.

Keisha watched her friends standing there. They were only two feet away from her, but it seemed like a whole world separated them. Neither Sarah nor Emily would look her in the eye. Emily just kept twisting her long brown hair around one finger while staring into the distance, and Sarah was fidgeting with the strap on her backpack.

"What's going on?" Jenna asked, returning to the hallway. Emily and Sarah turned to her and smiled. Now that Jenna was there, they seemed much more at ease.

"Nothing," Sarah said.

"Keisha just stopped by to say hi," Emily added.

Jenna's eyes scanned Keisha from top to bottom and back again. "Sarah and Emmy said they asked you to come to the movies this weekend but you said no. Why?"

You know why, Keisha thought, glaring at Jenna.

"We have a date for you and everything," she added, smirking.

"Right," Keisha said with a sneer. "Seth Carpenter."

"What's wrong with that?" Jenna asked, blinking innocently.

Keisha rolled her eyes. "He's a fourth grader," she said.

Jenna gave a little half shrug. "I figured that was about your speed," she said. Keisha glanced at Sarah and Emily, but they were both conveniently looking away again.

"What's that supposed to mean?" Keisha hissed.

"Whoa—take it easy. I'm just kidding," Jenna added with a smile. "So you don't want to sit with Seth. What about Tim? He'll probably be there, too. You could sit with him."

Both Emily's and Sarah's eyebrows shot up

into the air. They were obviously as surprised by Jenna's offer as Keisha was.

"Then would you come?" Jenna asked.

What—to sit with Tim Matheson? He may be a sixth grader, but he acts like a fourth grader. And besides, it didn't matter what boy Jenna offered up—Keisha wanted to go to the movies with her friends. And she wanted to be invited by her friends because they wanted her there, not because they needed to fill an empty seat.

"Well?" Jenna asked. "Would you?"

I'd rather sit home and pull out all my teeth, Keisha thought. "No," she said firmly.

Jenna shook her head and smirked. "I told you she wouldn't," she said to Emily and Sarah. "She's like totally scared of boys or something."

"That's not it," Keisha said.

"It's like I said at lunch the other day," Jenna went on. "She may be twelve, but she acts like she's ten."

Sarah and Emily snickered ever so slightly and Keisha whirled to face them. Neither of them seemed able to meet Keisha's eyes as they laughed at her, but that wasn't much of a consolation.

"Why do your friends not defend you?" Naeemah asked.

Keisha took one last look at Sarah and Emily, then turned and walked away. "Because they're not my friends anymore," she muttered. "That's why."

On her way to the art room, Keisha stopped in the girls' room to blow her nose and wipe away the tears that had started to form in her eyes.

"They are foolish," Naeemah said. "Immature and insensitive, if you ask me. Sam and Amanda are much more worthy of your friendship." Keisha knew that Naeemah was probably right, but she, Emily, and Sarah had been friends for so long that it was hard to let them go.

With a damp paper towel, Keisha dabbed at her eyes until the tickling sensation of nearly formed tears went away. Then she went to meet Amanda and Sam.

Today they were at work painting a large mural that included flags from numerous countries painted on a piece of cardboard. "That looks great," Keisha said, trying to sound cheerful.

"Keisha!" Amanda yelled. "I have awesome news!" Keisha was about to ask what it was, but she didn't get a chance. "I called my mom to tell her about the posters and to see if we should put any up here, and she said she talked to WGBH this afternoon and they're interested in covering the dance! We're going to be on TV!" Amanda said. She ran over to Keisha and grabbed her hands, jumping up and down. "Isn't that cool?" Amanda's enthusiasm was so overwhelming that Keisha found herself bouncing, too, although she still wasn't sure why.

"They want to interview us," Sam said over his shoulder. He was still working, despite Amanda's outburst.

"Wait—who?" Keisha asked when Amanda had finally stopped bouncing.

"*Us*," Amanda said. "Me, you, and Sam. They told my mom they wanted to talk to kids that were involved with planning the dance to get their take on it, and my mom said that since the three of us have been the most involved, we'll probably be the ones they interview."

"Wow," Keisha said, "that's really cool, but—" She paused to look at both Amanda and Sam. "Why me? I mean, the two of you have done a lot, but I've only been helping since yesterday."

"You better get to work, then," Sam said

without turning around. "I don't want to have to tell everyone who watches the six o'clock news that you're a slacker."

"Yeah," Amanda said with a giggle. "Grab a brush and get working. We've still got all of the African flags to finish."

Keisha glanced down at Naeemah, who was hiding in her shirt pocket, to see the small girl holding up two index fingers and smiling.

Thumbs, *Naeemah*, she thought. *It's thumbs up. Not index fingers.*

CHAPTER
Nine

"Are you really going to be inside that little box in the living room?" Naeemah asked.

"You mean the TV?"

"Yes, the . . . TV," Naeemah said tentatively.

Keisha nodded. "I think so."

"I still do not understand," Naeemah said, shaking her head. "They will have to make you my size in order to fit you in the box. How will that be done?"

Keisha snorted, trying unsuccessfully to stifle her laugh.

"Everything okay back there, Keisha?" Mrs. Johnson asked, turning down the minivan's radio. Keisha's mother had forbidden her to ride in the front seat ever since she'd heard that backseats were safer for kids. Usually, Keisha protested because riding in back made her feel like a little kid, but today she didn't mind because it made it easier to talk to Naeemah.

"Fine," Keisha replied. "I was just thinking of something funny that happened in school today."

Mrs. Johnson turned the radio back up and continued listening to talk radio while Keisha tried not to giggle at the idea of having to be shrunken in order to be on TV.

Keisha, Naeemah, and Mrs. Johnson were headed to the final planning meeting for the multicultural, multischool dance that was being held at Adams next week. Mrs. Johnson had gotten involved when Amanda called Keisha earlier to tell her about the meeting and invite her to come. According to Amanda's mom, the news crew from WGBH was going to be there, and if Amanda, Sam, and Keisha could all attend, it would be a convenient time for them to do the interview.

Amanda's mom had offered to pick up Keisha, but Mrs. Johnson had said that she'd be interested in attending. She wanted to see if there was anything she could do to help. She had some Brazilian art and Mexican pottery at her shop that she thought the school might want to borrow to use as decorations for the dance.

"I'm really glad you got involved in this,

Keisha," Mrs. Johnson said as she pulled into the school parking lot. "It's nice to see you trying new things, and this is a great cause. Linda Littlefield told me that the proceeds from the dance will help the PTO bring local artists to the schools to put on assemblies and do projects with the students. Isn't that great?"

"Yeah," Keisha replied. She'd heard all about that from Amanda, and it did sound cool, but right now she was more excited about the dance itself.

"I, too, am glad you have become involved," Naeemah said. "It has given you an opportunity to spend time with Amanda and Sam, and I quite like them. I do not think either of them would report me to a scientist."

"Probably not," Keisha agreed.

"Did you say something?" Mrs. Johnson asked, parking the car and pulling up the emergency brake.

"Nope, but there's Mrs. Littlefield's car. Amanda and Sam must already be here. I'm going inside, okay?" Keisha unbuckled herself and jumped out of the car before her mother had a chance to respond. She ran up the walkway toward the main entrance, excited to see Amanda and Sam and to get ready for their interview.

Once inside the school, she headed for the music room, where the meeting was being held. "Okay, hop in," Keisha said just outside the music room door. She held open the pocketbook she'd brought with her and Naeemah leaped inside.

Just then, Mrs. Johnson came around the corner. "Have you seen Amanda and Sam yet?" she asked.

"No, but I'm sure they're inside," Keisha said as she opened the music room door. She took three steps and stopped dead in her tracks. There at the front of the room, being interviewed by the WGBH news crew, was Jenna Scott with her two new BFF's: Sarah Robbins and Emily Reisman.

"Keisha, you didn't tell me Sarah and Emily were helping out with the dance," Mrs. Johnson said.

"I didn't know they were."

"Is that Amanda's mother?" Mrs. Johnson asked, pointing at a woman with a clipboard who seemed to be in charge. "I'm going to say hello. I haven't met her in person yet." Keisha nodded.

As Mrs. Johnson walked away, Amanda and Sam came to join Keisha.

"Are they—?" Keisha started.

"No," Amanda said.

"Then why—?"

"It's typical," Sam said. "Amanda and I have helped out with other PTO projects like this—the community garden behind the school, the Fourth of July teachers' dunk tank. Jenna's parents are always involved, but Jenna never shows up unless there's something in it for her."

"Like being on TV," Amanda said. "Her mom probably told her the news crew was going to be here tonight and that they wanted to interview some kids. My mom sent an e-mail out to the whole publicity committee to let them know."

"That bites!" Naeemah exclaimed, popping her head out of Keisha's bag again. To Keisha's surprise, both Amanda *and* Sam followed the sound of Naeemah's voice and spotted her peeking out at them.

"I told you I saw something, Sam!" Amanda exclaimed.

"I thought you were crazy," Sam replied, without taking his eyes off Naeemah.

"You guys can . . . *see* her?" Keisha asked, just as stunned as her two friends.

"Yes, they can! They can!" Naeemah

cheered, jumping up and down and clapping her hands.

"Where did . . . she come from?" Sam asked, still staring at the tiny figure.

"She popped out of a book of fairy tales," Keisha said.

"A book of fairy tales!" Amanda exclaimed. "I knew she looked familiar! Sam, that's the girl from—"

Sam clapped a hand over her mouth. "Shhh!"

"But, Sam, she's—"

"I don't care," he told her. "There's a news crew right over there, and if they see her, she's going to turn into a prime-time story."

"But—"

"No buts," Sam insisted.

Amanda exhaled heavily. "I guess you're right," she said. She turned to Keisha. "You promise to tell us everything later?"

"Uh, sure," Keisha said, staring at Amanda and Sam with surprise. She would have expected them to be a little more freaked out by Naeemah's presence, but they just seemed to accept that she was real without question. Then again, neither Amanda nor Sam was like anybody she'd ever met before.

"Okay," Amanda said, refocusing herself.

"Let's go. We have an interview to crash." Amanda started for the news crew, with Keisha and Sam following behind. They stopped just behind the camera and listened while Jenna, Emily, and Sarah answered questions for WGBH.

"What did you girls contribute to the project?" the reporter asked, placing the microphone in front of Jenna's mouth.

"I've been helping my mom deliver posters from the printer and stuff," Jenna said.

"And what about you two?" the reporter asked Emily and Sarah.

Sarah leaned toward the microphone and opened her mouth, but nothing came out. All she could do was stare at the camera, her eyes wide and unblinking.

"We're planning to go to the dance," Emily said finally. Then she froze up, too, just smiling and gazing straight ahead.

"Great," the reporter said after a minute. "Well, thank you very much for your time, ladies."

"You're welcome," Jenna said, granting him one of her winning-est smiles. "When did you say this will be on TV?"

"Sunday at six," the camerawoman replied.

"Cool. Thanks," Jenna said. She strode past

Keisha, Amanda, and Sam with a smug smile on her face. Sarah and Emily walked by without even acknowledging their presence.

"That was horrible," the camerawoman told the reporter. "I'm not sure we got anything we can use for our segment. They didn't even seem to know what the word *multicultural* meant."

Keisha clapped her hand to her mouth and giggled. So Jenna couldn't waltz in at the last minute and get all the glory! There *was* justice in the world. She glanced at Amanda and Sam, who were also grinning widely.

Amanda stepped forward and tapped the camerawoman on the elbow. "Excuse me," she said, "but my friends and I have been involved with this project for a while now. We could probably answer any questions you still have."

Both the camerawoman and the reporter turned around. "Here are some more kids. Should we try another interview?" the camerawoman asked.

The reporter looked skeptical. "What have *you* three contributed to this project?" he asked.

"We've been working on the decorations with Ms. Rainey, the art teacher," Amanda said. "She's having some of her classes take care of a lot of the small stuff—"

"Like strings of paper cranes to hang around the gym," Sam said, "and little cutouts of Earth to use as name tags."

"But we've working on the bigger things," Keisha jumped in. "Like palm trees and flags and—"

"Okay, okay," the reporter said. "You three are up. Come right over here with me and let Mindy get the camera ready. I'm going to ask you that question again so we can get your answers on tape, and then I'll go through the rest of them. All right?"

"Sure," Amanda, Keisha, and Sam answered together.

"Frigid!" Naeemah called out from Keisha's bag. "We are going to be in the little box in the living room!" The three friends all exchanged looks and then burst out laughing.

CHAPTER
Ten

To: keishaj123@ma.inet.com
From: jazzypdesigns@nh.teletron.com
Subject: re: thanks!

Keisha,
   I know exactly what you mean by "short."
Call me when you get this e-mail and we
can chat.

                    Jasmine

Keisha received the e-mail from Jasmine on
Saturday morning and called her right away.
Once Keisha finished telling Jasmine about
Naeemah and how she'd sprung out of a picture,
Jasmine filled her in on what had happened to

her and her three friends when they'd had the bracelet. It turned out that it was the bracelet that had been magic all along.

The first thing Keisha had done when she got off the phone with Jasmine was call Amanda and Sam. The three of them had gotten together for pizza that afternoon—with Naeemah, too, of course—and talked nonstop about pictures coming to life, the bracelet, and magic. The one thing they hadn't been able to figure out, though, was why Amanda and Sam were able to see Naeemah when no one else could.

Amanda said she had a theory, but that she needed to see the book Naeemah had come from to be certain. Unfortunately, she'd had to drive to Portland, Maine, with her parents right after pizza to visit an uncle, and she hadn't gotten back until late Sunday night. So the three friends had decided to go to Keisha's house after school on Monday so that Amanda could see the book and finally share her theory with them.

Now, sitting in Mrs. MacKnight's homeroom on Monday morning, Keisha could hardly wait for the afternoon to come.

She looked over at Amanda in the seat next to hers and smiled. Mrs. MacKnight's latest act of random kindness had been to tear up the old seating chart and allow students to choose their own desks for homeroom. Amanda had immediately snagged the one right next to Keisha and Naeemah, which had been easy to do because Keisha had been saving it for her.

Naeemah lay stretched out on her stomach on Keisha's desk, her legs bent upward and her head cradled in her hands. For Naeemah, the best thing about having two new confidants was that she no longer had to hide out in Keisha's bag, backpack, or shirt pockets.

For Keisha, there were two benefits. For one thing, she didn't have to worry about keeping Naeemah's remarkable appearance to herself. And for another, she had two new best friends.

"I wish I could fit on the desk like that," Amanda said, pointing at Naeemah. "These chairs stink."

Naeemah turned around and began sniffing the air. "I do not smell anything," she said.

Both Keisha and Amanda giggled. "It's not that they actually smell, Neema," Keisha whispered. "We just don't like them. They're not comfortable."

"*Neema*," Amanda murmured. "I like that."

"I do, too," Naeemah said with a smile. "It will be my new knickknack."

"*Name*. Nick*name*," Keisha corrected.

"I love the way she talks," Amanda laughed.

"You should have seen her watching the news last night. When it showed us talking to Pat Cameron about the dance, she went crazy. She kept jumping up and down and asking how I could be here and there, big and small, all at once. It took me all night to explain."

"Things are very different here," Naeemah said with a bit of a pout.

Amanda and Keisha exchanged concerned glances. "We're sorry, Neema," Amanda said. "We're not laughing *at* you."

"No way," Keisha agreed. "It's just that some of the things you say come out funny. But you shouldn't be embarrassed. You're doing way better here than I would in ancient Egypt."

"Me, too," Amanda agreed.

Naeemah studied both of their faces extensively, then smiled. "Thank you," she said. "I believe that is true."

Keisha crinkled her nose and looked at Amanda. "Did she just slam us?" she asked, but Amanda didn't have a chance to answer.

"Okay, class," Mrs. MacKnight called, flicking off the lights. "Let's all watch the TV. We have a special announcement this morning."

Amanda raised her eyebrows at Keisha, who shrugged. It wasn't often that they got video announcements—usually only when a sports team had done really well and made it into the news.

That's it, Keisha thought. "The news!" she exclaimed as the picture came into focus on the TV.

"You are in the little box again!" Naeemah called, staring at the small television mounted above Mrs. MacKnight's desk. Sure enough, there was Keisha along with Amanda and Sam, being interviewed by Pat Cameron of WGBH news. Mrs. MacKnight told the class that the station had sent a copy of the segment to the principal so she could play to help advertise the dance.

"So tell me what's going to be different about this dance?" Pat Cameron asked.

"Well, for one thing," Keisha replied, "it's not just for Adams. All of the area middle schools have been invited, so there will be a lot more students there."

"Yeah, and the theme of this dance is multi-culturalism," Amanda added.

"What does that mean?" the reporter asked.

"It means that a lot of different cultures will be represented," Sam said.

"There are students from a lot of different countries in our district," Amanda went on.

"Sudan, the Dominican Republic, Poland, Thailand—"

"—Somalia, India, Lebanon," Keisha added. "The point of this dance is to bring all of the students in our district together to celebrate our differences."

"Do you have any idea how many different countries will be represented at this dance?" the reporter asked.

"I think there are something like fifty," Sam said.

"Yeah, that's about right," Amanda agreed. "But this isn't just going to be a dance," she added.

"It isn't?" the reporter asked.

"No," Keisha jumped in. "There are going to be other things going on, too. Like there will be food from a lot of different countries—"

"And there's going to be a drumming workshop," Sam added.

"And belly-dancing lessons," Amanda put in.

As the interview continued to play on the TV, students began turning to Amanda and Keisha as though they were impressed to have such celebrities in their presence. And when it was over, they all crowded around the two girls to ask questions.

"What time does the dance start?"

"How much does it cost to get in?"

"Do you really think there will be a lot of kids from other schools there?"

Amanda and Keisha could barely keep up with them, and when the bell rang and they made their way into the hall, things only got worse. People were approaching Amanda and Keisha left and right, some just to tell them that the dance sounded cool and others to find out if there was anything they could do to help.

Jenna, Emily, and Sarah were hanging out near the water fountain. Jenna was trying to look bored and uninterested, but her face was bright red. Emily and Sarah just stood there fidgeting. None of them would make eye contact with Keisha.

When the girls finally arrived at their lockers, which, thanks to their last names—Johnson and Littlefield—were pretty close together, Amanda pulled out a bunch of posters advertising the dance.

"Hey, Keisha, you want to help me with these?" she asked.

"Sure," Keisha replied, taking half the stack from her arms.

"Let me see that," someone said, grabbing a poster from Keisha's hand.

"Hey—it is the *hottie*!" Naeemah exclaimed gleefully. "I must say, for a twelve-year-old, he is rather smoking."

Keisha turned to see that it was, indeed, Noah Carpenter. As he read the poster, Keisha took a moment to look him over. His curly black hair, which had always seemed so out of control to her before, now seemed to make a kind of dark halo above his head. And his deep brown eyes, which had always seemed so cruel and mocking to her, looked more thoughtful and intelligent than she remembered. *I guess it's been a while since I've looked at him,* Keisha thought.

"Cool," he said, handing the poster back to Keisha. Her heart did a little flip-flop as his hand grazed hers, and Keisha swallowed hard. *What was that about?*

"Well? Are you going to go?" Amanda demanded.

"I don't know. Are *you*?" he asked Keisha.

"Me?" Keisha replied. What did he care what *she* was going to do? "Well, yeah. I mean, I'm helping with all the decorations and everything, so . . . I guess I'll be there."

Noah turned back to Amanda. "Yeah, I'll probably go," he said.

"No-ah," came a singsong voice from over

Keisha's shoulder. "You're going to be late for math class." It was Jenna Scott, with Emily and Sarah right behind her, of course.

"I gotta go to class," Noah said. "Later," he added, looking directly at Keisha. She felt like she was going to melt. Noah gave her a sideways smile, then trotted off to join Jenna and her flock.

"Whoa," Amanda said once Noah was gone. "Someone's got a crush."

Keisha's eyebrows shot upward. "What?! I do not. I was only talking to him because—"

"Not *you*. *Him*," Amanda said.

Keisha turned just in time to see Noah, Jenna, and the others disappear around the corner. "Are you kidding?" she asked, whirling on Amanda.

"Are you blind?" Amanda shot back.

Keisha looked to Naeemah for support, but Naeemah had a strange smile on her face. "I observed it as well," she said. "He was totally macking on you."

"He was not!" Keisha exclaimed.

"You can think what you want," Amanda replied, "but I thought it was pretty obvious."

Keisha felt her stomach rise into her chest like she was having a falling dream. "Do you really think so?" she asked, a strange sense of excitement building inside her. "What . . . what should I do?"

Amanda shrugged. "You don't have to do anything."

"Even in my culture, you would not need to think about marriage for at least another year," Naeemah put in. "Perhaps two."

Keisha rolled her eyes. "Thanks, Neema. That helps a lot."

"I knew it!" Amanda exclaimed suddenly, staring at Naeemah. "You *are* from that book, aren't you?"

"I am from *a* book," Naeemah replied. "But of which book are you speaking?"

Amanda sighed. "I was going to wait until we were all at your house together, but . . . " She looked from Keisha to Naeemah and back again. "I can't wait anymore. It's a book of fairy tales that my grandmother used to have. When I was little, I used to read it every time I was over at her house, and there was this one story I always loved about an Egyptian girl who runs away from her village so she won't have to get married."

"That is *my* story!" Naeemah cried.

"I know," Amanda said. "You look just like the girl in the picture, floating down the river on that raft with the two crocodiles—"

"That's the picture she came out of!" Keisha exclaimed.

"Oh, my gosh. I loved that picture so much that I made a color photocopy of it and put it up in my room. I still have it. And every time Sam comes over, he takes it down and looks at it. He wants to be an illustrator someday, and he's always talking about how real that picture looks—like the girl could just . . . *walk right out of it*," she finished, gaping at Naeemah.

"Your grandmother must have the same book that I have," Keisha said.

Amanda's face went from total excitement to absolute dismay. "No. She moved into a condo last year and ended up giving away a bunch of her stuff. She didn't know how much I loved the book or she would have given it to me. Instead, most of her stuff went to some antique dealer who said he'd find a place for it all."

Keisha's eyes lit up. "An antique dealer?" she asked, but before Amanda could respond, the bell rang, making them officially late for language arts.

"We better get going," Amanda said. "Mr. Coggins will give us detentions if we're too late."

"Okay," Keisha said, "but you, me, and Sam are heading *straight* to my house after school. We have a lot to talk about."

CHAPTER
Eleven

"Oh, my gosh! This is my grandmother's book!" Amanda cried as she flipped open the front cover of *Faerie Tales* in Keisha's bedroom. "I can tell from the inscription: *For Louise, with love, Mom and Dad*," she said. "But how did you end up with it?"

Keisha, Amanda, Sam, and Naeemah were all gathered in Keisha's room to look at the book.

"It was at my mom's shop," Keisha said. "As soon as you told me your grandmother's stuff went to an antique dealer, I remembered that my mom had said she got all kinds of new books, including this one, from an antique dealer who was going out of business. It was probably the same guy."

"Whoa," Sam said. "That's wild."

"So, do you think that's why we can see

Neema, too?" Amanda asked. "Because of the book and the picture in my room?"

"That has to be it," Keisha said. "What else could it be?"

"Yeah," Sam agreed. "I think Keisha's right. We read that story a lot when we were kids. Amanda insisted on reading it out loud every time I went to visit her grandmother with her."

Amanda scowled at him. "You liked it, too, Sam," she said.

"Well, sure. It's a good story. Especially the part where you cured that guy on the side of the river and he ended up being the pharaoh's vizier."

Naeemah jumped up and squealed. "You know the end of my story?" she asked.

"Yeah," Sam replied. "Don't you?"

"The pages were torn out," Keisha said, "and all Neema remembers is floating down the river for a really long time."

"Ohmigosh! I almost forgot!" Amanda said. "My little brother tore those pages out years ago. He lost his allowance for two weeks because of that. And the little rat flushed them down the toilet, so there was no way to tape them back in or anything."

"So you've just been floating down the river all this time?" Sam asked.

"I believe so," Naeemah replied. "But please, tell me how my story ends."

"Hmmm," Amanda said. "Let's see, you ran away and you were drifting down the river for a while, but then you decided you couldn't leave your family behind and that you'd have to find a way to be a doctor in your own village. But then—help me out here, Sam. What happened next?"

"She got the raft over to the side of the river somehow—because you were going to walk back," he told Naeemah, "but then that's where you found that man lying in the grass."

"Right," Amanda said. "There was this guy who was all bent over, and he was moaning and stuff. I can't remember what was wrong with him, but you knew enough about medicine to help him out. You got him some herbs and put a cool cloth on his head and stuff, and eventually, after a few days, he got better."

"And it turned out that he was actually the pharaoh's vizier!" Sam added excitedly.

"What's a vizier?" Keisha asked.

"That's the pharaoh's right-hand man," Sam explained. "And he was so grateful to Neema for helping him that he told her he would give her any gift she named."

"And you told him you wanted to study to be

a doctor," Amanda said. "So he made it happen."

"And did I return to my family?" Naeemah asked.

Amanda nodded. "Mm-hm. And a few years later, when you were practicing medicine, you married a scribe who'd helped you out a lot."

"Siamun?" Naeemah breathed.

"I don't remember his name," Amanda said.

"Oh, but it has to be Siamun!" Naeemah cried. "I have loved him for all of my girlhood! And with him as my husband, I know I could fulfill all of my dreams. He knows my wishes, and he shares them!"

"That's *so* romantic," Amanda gushed. "Just like Keisha and Noah."

"Amanda!" Keisha said, swatting at her friend.

"You and Noah Carpenter?" Sam asked. "Since when?"

"Since never," Keisha barked. Thankfully, Naeemah interrupted before Amanda could say anything else.

"I must get back to my family—and to Siamun. I must finish my story so that I can pursue my dreams." She ran to the book, which was open in Amanda's lap, and began jumping up and down on the picture, trying to get back into it.

"Oh, no! It won't work!" she cried. "I'll never get back to my life now!" Naeemah threw herself down on the page and began sobbing while Keisha, Sam, and Amanda looked on.

It was the first time Keisha had seen the tiny girl lose her composure. "It's all right, Neema," she said, stroking the tiny figure's back with the tip of her index finger. "We'll find a way to get you back." She looked to Amanda and Sam for help.

"It seems to me," Sam said after a moment, "that if the bracelet is what brought her out of the book, the bracelet is what's going to get her back in."

"Yeah," Amanda agreed. "Think, Keisha. What happened just before Neema came out of the book? Did you make a wish on the bracelet or anything?"

Keisha pressed her eyes shut and tried to recall the moment exactly as it had happened. "I don't think so," she said. "I just reached down to touch the picture, and then there was this bright flash. And when I looked back at the book, Neema was gone."

"You reached down to touch the picture?" Sam asked. Keisha nodded. "Show us how."

"Do it exactly the same," Amanda instructed.

"Okay," Keisha said. She picked up the book

and sat down on her bed with it, trying to position herself and it exactly as they had been. "I think it was like this," she said. Slowly, she reached down with her left hand, aiming for the spot where Naeemah had been standing. As she did, her bracelet grazed the picture and something remarkable happened. "Look, you guys!" Keisha yelled.

Sam, Amanda, and Naeemah gathered around the page and stared down at the illustration. With the touch of the bracelet, the picture had gone liquid, all of the colors swirling around on the page.

"I think this is it!" Keisha said, gazing at Naeemah. "It looks like all you have to do is . . . jump in."

Naeemah nodded. She looked over at Keisha and smiled, a small tear rolling down her cheek. "I am most desirous to get back to my village," she said, "but I shall miss you and your new friends dearly."

"I'm going to miss you, too," Keisha said, realizing her own eyes were beginning swell.

Just then, Naeemah removed her necklace from around her head and took a stone off the middle of it. It was a glass bead, brown with gold tones. "This is a tiger's-eye," Naeemah said, handing Keisha the bead. "It belonged to my great-grandmother, and it has been handed down in my family for generations."

"I can't take this," Keisha said.

"I wish for you to have it," Naeemah said. "Consider it blang-blang to help you remember me."

Keisha took the bead and chuckled, wiping away a tear. "Bling-bling," she said.

"Ah, yes, bling-bling," the tiny Egyptian said, laughing with her. "I shall always cherish the interesting words you have taught me."

"And I will always remember you—with or without the bling-bling," Keisha said. Then, remembering Naeemah's custom, she bowed low to the small Egyptian girl and smiled. Naeemah grinned and bowed in return. Then she said good-bye to Sam and Amanda, and took a running leap at the picture.

All of a sudden, there was a blinding flash, and when they looked again, Naeemah was standing back where each of them had originally seen her—on the raft, floating down the river, with a crocodile on either side. Only this time, Keisha noted, instead of looking so melancholy, Naeemah appeared to be smiling.

CHAPTER
Twelve

"That is *so* cool!" Sam said, watching the drummers who had come to perform at the multicultural dance. There was a group of five men called African Rhythms and they were drawing quite a crowd.

"How does he do that?" Keisha asked as one of the men played a set of eight conga drums, alternating between using his fingertips, flat palms, and the heels of his hands so fast that she could barely follow his movements.

"It's awesome!" Amanda said.

The three friends watched in awed silence as two other drummers joined in on congas to add to the rhythm, and the two remaining members of the group chimed in on some ancient looking bronze bells and rattles made of giant gourds covered with nets of beads.

"Woohoo!" someone in the crowd cheered, and others whistled and applauded as the rhythm sped up and grew more intense. Keisha glanced at the crowd around her, pleased to see so many smiling faces. The turnout for the dance had been greater than anyone had expected. There were more than two hundred students there from Adams alone. With all of the other schools included, the attendance was probably around eight hundred.

When the drumming finally stopped, the crowd went wild with applause—but the excitement was just beginning. Before the applause could die down, a DJ at the side of the stage powered up her sound system, filling the gymnasium with the deep bass of a popular hip-hop tune. The students went wild again, jumping up and down to the beat.

Caught up in the excitement, Keisha grinned at her friends and busted out an exaggerated version of a dance move she'd seen in a music video. Both Sam and Amanda burst out laughing, so Keisha launched into a routine she still remembered from a street funk class her mother had enrolled her in when she was eight. She was midway through "the butterfly" when someone behind her called out. "Nice moves!"

Keisha froze. She knew that voice. Slowly, she turned to her left to see—who else?—Noah Carpenter. *Oh, man, why did he have to see me do that?* she thought, feeling her cheeks heat up. She looked to her friends for support, but Sam was oblivious and Amanda only smirked at her.

"Hey, Sam!" Amanda shouted over the music. "Let's go get some *pupusas*!"

Sam screwed up his face. "Some what?"

"*Pupusas*," Amanda repeated. Then she grabbed him by the arm. "Come here, I'll show you," she said, dragging him toward the food tables.

Oh, great, Keisha thought. *Alone with Noah Carpenter.* She smiled awkwardly at him and tried to think of something to say, but her mind was blank.

"The dance is really cool," he said.

"What, the *butterfly*?" Keisha asked, surprised. "I was just fooling around. It's not—"

"No, I mean the *dance*. *This* dance," Noah said, indicating the entire gymnasium with his hand. "A lot of people showed up."

"Oh, right," Keisha said, feeling even more foolish. She fidgeted with her charm bracelet, grasping for the the tiger's-eye Naeemah had given her. With her mother's help, she'd managed to affix it to the charm bracelet right between the unicorn and the princess. "Yeah, it seems to be going well."

Noah nodded. "Those drummers were cool. And the decorations look really good. Which ones did you help with?"

"Me? Oh, I . . . um—" Keisha swallowed hard. Why was she having such a hard time putting complete sentences together? She rolled the tiger's-eye between her thumb and forefinger and scanned the gym. "I helped paint the Taj Mahal, over there," she said, pointing. "And that tree, and the elephant, and I drew most of the flags, too. And those people dancing. Actually," she continued as she looked around, "I guess I helped with most of the decorations. Wow. I didn't realize I'd done so much," she added in a low voice, talking more to herself than to Noah.

"You're a really good artist," he said.

Keisha felt her stomach flutter. She smiled and stared down at her feet. "Thanks." She wasn't quite sure what it was, but there was something about Noah that made her feel both embarrassed and excited all at once. It was sort of a scary feeling, but at the same time it was nice, too. "I've always liked drawing. I—"

"Noah! I've been looking all over for you," Jenna said, bursting into the conversation. She walked right up to him and put her arm around his shoulders. "There's a drum workshop in the music room. Justin, Luke, Emily, and Sarah are saving seats for us."

The fluttering sensation in Keisha's stomach came to an abrupt halt and turned into more of a churning feeling. Jenna's presence tended to have that effect.

"Cool," Noah said, and Keisha felt a sudden wave of disappointment. Why did Jenna always have to show up and ruin things?

"Well?" Jenna said, shifting her weight to her left leg. "What are you waiting for? Let's go."

She gave Noah a little tug, but Noah took a step away from her, allowing her arm to fall back to her side. "I'll be there in a minute," he said.

Jenna raised one eyebrow and glanced from him to Keisha and back again. "It's starting like, right now," she said.

"So go ahead," Noah told her. "I'll catch up."

Keisha's stomach went right back to fluttering. Was Noah actually going to stay and talk to her instead of running off with Jenna?

Apparently, Jenna was wondering the same thing. For a moment, she stood frozen, looking at Noah like he had three heads. Then she narrowed her eyes and gave Keisha a glare that could have been accompanied by lightning bolts. "Fine," Jenna snapped. "But don't take too long or you'll lose your seat." Then she turned and stomped away.

"Whoa," Keisha said. "I think she's a little upset with you."

Noah shook his head. "Nah. That's just the way Jenna talks. She's intense."

"Yeah, I guess," Keisha agreed, although *intense* probably wasn't the word she would have used.

"So, are you going to the drumming thing?" Noah asked, nodding after Jenna.

"No," Keisha said. "I went to the earlier one."

Noah pressed his lips together, creating a dimple on one side. "Oh," he said, and he actually sounded disappointed. Could Amanda have been right? Could he actually *like* her? As more than a friend?

"Well, I better get going. Before I lose my seat," Noah said with a smirk.

"Yeah," Keisha agreed, smiling.

Noah started to walk away, then turned around and grinned at her. "Hey, if you're still here when I get back, maybe you can show me how to do that moth dance," he teased.

Keisha covered her face and shook her head. "It's the *butterfly*," she said, giggling.

"Whatever," Noah said with a smile. Then he turned and jogged out of the gym.

In a matter of seconds, Amanda was back at Keisha's side. "So he *doesn't* have a crush on you, huh?" she said.

Keisha shrugged her shoulders. She wasn't sure what to believe.

"He was totally flirting with you," Amanda continued. "You'd have to be blind not to see it."

A smile crept across Keisha's face. It was an incredible feeling to be recognized for her hard work on the dance, and she was sharing that recognition with two new friends—who, in just a few weeks, had made her feel more secure about herself than Sarah and Emily ever had. And now Noah was pleasantly surprising her, as well. He was actually quite sincere after all, and not as easily blinded by Jenna's popularity as Keisha had presumed. She wished Naeemah were there to share this satisfying moment with her, but she knew that the little Egyptian girl was reveling in dreamlike moments of her own, and happy again in her own world.

Get Ready for Charm Club
Book #6:
water sapphire

"And finally," Mrs. MacKnight said, reaching the end of the afternoon announcements, "any sixth grader wishing to run for the student council seat vacated by Madeleine Heimburg must submit an application to Mr. Hupp by three P.M. this afternoon. That's about fifteen minutes from now."

Madeleine Heimburg had been voted in as a sixth-grade student council representative at the beginning of the year, along with Jason Poole. In fact, they'd been the only two to run for the seats back in September. But Maddie was transferring to a private school in Vermont for the second half of the year, which meant that her seat was open. And Amanda Littlefield wanted it.

"I wonder who else is going to run," Amanda murmured, glancing around the room.

"What do you mean, *who else*?" Keisha asked. "Do you know someone who *is*?"

"Yes," Amanda said with a nod. "Me."

Keisha's eyebrows arched upward. "*You*?"

"Is there something wrong with that?" Amanda asked.

"No," Keisha said, "not at all. I just didn't know you were interested."

"Of course I'm interested," Amanda replied. "I can't just sit back and let a bunch of gingerbread people run our school." Just then the bell rang. "So do you want to come with me?"

"Where?" Keisha asked.

"To Mr. Hupp's room," Amanda said. "To turn in my application." Instead of waiting for Keisha to respond, Amanda grabbed her by the hand. "Come on," she said. "And then we'll find Sam and we can go hang out at your mom's shop."

"Okay," Keisha said, and the two friends made their way down the hall to their math teacher's room.

Mr. Hupp taught math to sixth, seventh, and eighth graders, and he was one of the most popular teachers in the school. His room was always filled with students after school, but it seemed especially busy today.

Amanda pushed her way through a mob of

boys who were wrestling just outside the door. "Why do guys always have to push one another around?" she asked.

"Because we have a lot of physical energy," Sam answered. "At least that's what my mom says."

"Sam! What are you doing here?" Amanda asked.

"Looking for you guys," Sam replied. "But I expected to find you at your lockers. What are you doing way down here in the eighth-grade hall?"

"Turning in Amanda's student council application," Keisha said. "Madeleine Heimburg is transferring and Amanda's running for her seat."

Sam's eyes opened wide. "You're running for student council?" he asked.

Amanda huffed. "Why does everybody sound so surprised?" She made her way into Mr. Hupp's room with Sam and Keisha following behind.

"I'm not . . . *surprised*," Sam said. "It's just— I mean—when did you decide to run? I didn't know you were the student council type."

Amanda took one look at the group gathered around Mr. Hupp's desk and turned back toward the door. "I'm not," she said.

"What?" Keisha said. "You just told me—"

"Forget what I told you," Amanda replied,

making her way back into the hall. "I just saw who else is running for the sixth grade, and I don't stand a chance."

"What are you talking about?" Keisha asked. "Of course you—"

"Keisha?" Jenna interrupted, walking out of Mr. Hupp's room. "Are you running for student council?"

Keisha rolled her eyes. "No," she said. "But Amanda is."

Jenna turned her attention to Amanda, giving her a quick up-and-down scan. "*You're* running?"

Amanda sighed. She'd had about enough of the shocked responses to the idea of her running. "What do you care?" she asked. Unfortunately, at the same time, both Sam and Keisha blurted out, "Yeah—she's running."

Jenna smirked at Emily and Sarah, who were flanking her, as usual. "That's even better," she said with a laugh. "What's your campaign platform? All-black school uniforms?" Jenna laughed at her own joke, and Sarah and Emily—being perfect carbon copies of their new leader—laughed, too.

Amanda watched them walk down the hallway, still giggling, and groaned. "She makes me so mad," she said.

"Don't let her get to you, Amanda," Keisha said. "We'll be the ones laughing when the election's over."

"Yeah," Sam agreed.

Amanda turned toward her friends, her hands on her hips. "No, we won't," she said. "Don't you guys get it? I can't beat Jenna Scott."

"Sure you can!" Keisha said.

"You'd be a much better student council rep than she would," Sam added.

"That doesn't matter," Amanda said. "I can't win more votes than her. She's way too popular, and I'm way too . . . *not*."

"But that's not fair," Keisha objected.

"That's life," Amanda replied. She held up her application form and looked at it. "I might as well just tear this thing up. It would take a miracle for me to win."

"A miracle?" Sam said, his eyes twinkling. "How about a little magic?"

Amanda scowled. "What are you talking about?"

"The bracelet!" Sam said, pointing to the silver chain on Keisha's wrist. "It brought Neema out of a picture book. I'm sure it could do something to help you win this election."

Amanda narrowed her eyes. "Like what? Stuff the ballot box?"

"I don't know," Sam said with a shrug. "There's got to be something."

"Thanks, Sam, but—"

"Sam's right," Keisha said. "We have this bracelet, and we know it's done amazing things before. Why not see if it can help again?"

Amanda shook her head. "I just don't think there's any way—"

"Sorry," Keisha interrupted. She unhooked the bracelet from her wrist and clasped it around Amanda's. "Too late. I'm passing the bracelet on to you. And I know it will bring you good luck," she added with a grin.

Amanda glanced down at the bracelet on her wrist. It now had five charms attached—the angel, the unicorn, the fairy, the princess, and the tiger's-eye that Naeemah had given to Keisha.

Good luck? Amanda thought as she touched the chain. She wondered if it was going to be enough.